Love in the RV Park

Jeffrey Ross

Published by
Rogue Phoenix Press
Copyright © 2013

ISBN: 978-1-62420-057-1

Credits

Cover Artist: Designs by Ms G
Editor: Christine Young

Printed in the United States of America

Oh What a Quirky Web We Weave
Foolish Tales of Love to Believe

The Little Colorado River Band in 1985

Dedication

To Jack Frost—a man of the forest and high desert, a terrific poet has struggled mightily with romantic impulses, yet finds happiness in graceful and creative solitude.

Adam Swiss
Singer/Songwriter

Adam Swiss sat on a bar stool and watched the cold late autumn rain drip pitifully off the corrugated patio cover. He noticed his old Yamaha, a 1969 DT-1 250 cc motorcycle, was staying dry under the tree where he'd parked it. The dented but clean motorcycle looked oddly misplaced in time, almost baleful, in the mists.

Tonight's crowd was thin on this creaky Moonbucks porch. Most of the patrons sat, isolated, hooded, completely inside the building, eyes glued to laptop screens or smart phones.

These poor !@#$% look like locusts stuck to plastic trees, thought Swiss to himself.

Swiss was here tonight, like the last three Friday nights, to provide background guitar music for the gathered coffee snobs. Moonbucks corporate policy forbade payment to musicians, but he would be given free coffee and cakes for the following week as payment in kind. But not even a gift card, he considered wryly.

Not so long ago, Swiss had been working at a college in the Midwest. Happily married, or so the town thought, he and his wife had been living the playful small community existence. Two cars, bundled cable and internet service, Friday night happy hours, and her new tattoos.

Now tattoos themselves weren't a problem to Swiss. But, madam butterfly had become a sparrow, then a raven, as Phyllis added twenty-five and later fifty pounds.

Soon she was so large she couldn't fit into size twenty-six pants.

Swiss was an educated man—a man who had great aesthetic sensibility. When romance became displaced by Kostco, snacks, and cooking shows blaring away 24/7 in his bedroom, he expressed concern. When he couldn't get his arms around his loving wife any more, he oiled the bike's chain. When the scale broke at home and she cussed him like a trooper, he'd had enough.

They didn't own any kids, and the shaky couple had even less money. He finally capitulated, gassed up his Yamaha DT-1, cleaned the spark plug, threw on a backpack, strapped on his guitar, and eventually rode six hundred tough, cold miles to Hamilton City, North New Mexico.

Adam Swiss was now living in a run-down forty-year-old travel trailer in an RV park on a low hill by the river, just off Edison Avenue. The trailer had heat, running water, and a shower. Sometimes the roof leaked during a rainstorm.

He had worked out a deal with management. He'd function as the on-site "go to guy" and do minor fixes and repairs for the other fifty-one residents of this five bar resort. In return, his rent was a nominal one hundred dollars monthly.

Swiss had no other job, and he was using his weekly Moonbucks gig as a way to hopefully advertise himself as a musician. He knew something good was ahead, just waiting to happen. He couldn't sing worth a lick, but he played guitar and bass pretty well.

What Swiss didn't know was that his density, uh—destiny, had forcefully and confidently walked into Moonbucks, wearing Capris pants, hair ribbons, pale lipstick, and church-recommended garments of restriction.

Her new pearl necklace and wedding ring sparkled first-class, and his feelings at that moment reminded old Swiss of those turgid emotions he once endured when a beautiful girl caught his eye for the very first time.

She sat down with three other well-heeled gals and ordered a glass of water and a chocolate muffin. They launched into a discussion of vampire novels, *American Idol,* and the next church social. Swiss busied himself tuning his guitar, which was rapidly going sharp in the damp air.

But his eyes were fixed on her curves, her presence, and her chattiness. And she was thin. And beautiful. And shining, by heaven, in the dim light.

The diamond-encrusted cross she wore, suspended from a loose, sensuous, silver chain, reflected stage lighting like a disco ball.

Now Swiss had been emotionally beaten, many times, under the roof of his old domicile. His manly wife had set him straight on most issues—especially on how couples should behave in public and in private. His wife had always been impressed by windbags, Dallas Cowboy jerseys, tats, and sports collectibles. But she had little respect for Adam.

He wanted so badly to have romantic feelings, to write love songs, to bring flowers, to feel the throb and pulse of fulfilled love and the gentle touch of a woman's willing lips.

So—Swiss, in an emotionally fragile state, broke, sort of on the lam, tired, and psychologically beaten, had been smitten instantly by this beautiful, curvy, nicely-dressed, clearly-married and socially-integrated woman. What would he do?

Well. He sat on the stool and caught snatches of the girls' conversations. He was trying to glean some significance, some meaning, some awful portent, and some transient mystic symbolism, for why their paths were crossing here. Not much came through.

Finally, in the Key of G, Adam Swiss broke into song, strumming his slightly amplified Rickenbacker 330 in the dim glow of the nearly romantic stage lights:

Are you waiting there for me—
While the light breaks from my Rickenbacker?
Are you thinking bits of me—
Making my life tick a little faster?
Are you dreaming? Are you mine?
Can you help my places grow and nourish?
Did you drive those miles for me?
And never sleep a wink 'cause
We were loving...
Did you wander to the sea—taking photos of the sunsets
    flooding?
Are you certain of your heart—and the life ahead you think of
    starting?
Tender moments come from always parting...
Can't we be, just what we are?

Two fates a-pounding on this middle class star
Can't we be, just what we seem?
Afraid of nothing but the happiness dream?

(At this point, some credit should be given to the obscure eighties rock quartet, The Rockhardz, who helped to craft this self-absorbed song.)

Leah Free
A Looker

Leah Free, meanwhile, nicely packaged and smelling very good, was heavily involved in a discussion about dill pickles, Christmas potlucks, and pantry odors. She did not fidget nor talk without listening. Mrs. Free had always boasted her ankles were her best attribute—and she gazed at her painted toenails and smoothly shaven legs with obvious satisfaction.

She also gazed at the balding-though-athletic singer. Closely. And the song made her smile—even if he were off key just a bit. She played piano for her church and knew about such things.

Leah Free was a beautiful woman. She knew how to dress and carry herself. Few would believe she had borne three sons. It's as if the cosmetic and fashion companies were invented for her. Everything fit, everything smelled great on her. Leah's exquisite and yet girlish figure was envied by most of her friends. Leah was clever and witty (B.A. in English from Copperfield Community College Super+ Program) and charming.

She had been married for twenty-two years to a good solid

citizen. Luther was an accountant at the local Go Green Power Plant—
he made d—- good money, was a successful investor and business
manager, had no bad habits, and was quite faux-athletic. He played
softball on Monday night, bowled on Tuesdays, went to church
Wednesday evenings, played in a Scrabble league on Thursdays, and
attended Bible studies with his church Men's Group on Fridays.

Leah's sons were excellent students. They were scholars, athletes,
and demonstrated only perfect behavior. Leah kept an immaculate
house—thanks to a salaried house keeper—and she drove a 2013 Lexus
SUV with over-sized black powder coat wheels, received a pedicure
thrice a week, and was encouraged to travel with her girlfriends by her
husband.

Certainly a common and clear-cut case of Subsidy.

Sometimes she felt guilty about the cost of her new bosom. But
not for very long. Her clothes fit so much better, and she was frequently
the center of attention wherever she went.

Even so. To the point. Despite all the accoutrements of success,
beauty, and a sophisticated life style, Leah was bored out of her mind.
She had been suffocated by a senseless and inadequate suburban prison.
How many more Christmas parties could she stand? How many ladies'
book discussion groups could she host? How many dental and vision
appointments must be arranged? Always church and church meetings,
always doctrine and potlucks. And board games!

Scrapbooking? Cooking? Cleaning? Maintaining the stucco barn
for unappreciative children?

Oil changes, lunch meetings, manicures, haircuts, vampire novels,
Harry Potter, school fund raisers, Little League, church twice a week,
card parties, date night (once every six months), golf lessons, bikini

waxes, birthdays. What was the sum of all?

Her good looks had brought her upper-middle-class status in a stale and stuffy land.

Her husband, with a crisp crew cut, was a strange automaton who had the future clearly mapped and always did the right thing. But Luther had no sense of past or present. He had money and stuff, but he was actually dumber than dirt.

She, to him, was a household appliance, a trophy, a doll.

Leah had thought about leaving her husband and kids, renting an apartment, reading A. R. Ammons poetry and maybe getting a little job at the Blue Caboose Diner as a server or something to pay the rent.

But she could not act on any such impulse. Her subsidized life was too good. Her shiny Lexus SUV was too nice, her charge cards had federal budget-sized limits, and she could not disrespect the social furniture which surrounded her and gave her credibility.

She had come so far from the twelve by sixty single wide (with an awning and skirting) of her youth. Her implants (giving her nearly perfect form) were priceless.

She and Mr. Crew Cut had timeshares, investments, an apartment building, rental properties, a boat, and more.

Leah's mother had never understood her complaints about Luther. "He is a good provider," her mom had said on more than one occasion. "That first husband of yours was a no-good bum!"

True enough, Leah thought, but first husband Michael could play guitar and sing like John Hiatt, and he could make love like Fabio after a drunken banquet! He didn't have a nickel, but he had, uh, style. And several motorcycles.

Her first husband was a "party-animal" who drank too much,

played bad guitar in a "wanna be" heavy metal band, chased skirts, and shunned the church scene.

He was always in the mood for love and would bring her flowers, usually after his drunken binges and inappropriate antics. But he was a real man and made no excuses.

Leah, to this day, held it as an absolute truth that the decay of their marriage was his entire fault.

Oh well. Just last week, she heard her ex had been arrested for vagrancy on the Santa Monica Beach. Apparently, Mike had been sleeping in an old refrigerator box and living off crabs he caught just off shore.

Rock on, Husband One. We should all be so lucky!

Leah's flesh and form were perfect, but she was not content. Under the skin, well, she had become a pedicured zombie. Nonetheless, enough of humanity still resided, still pulsed and throbbed, in her perky upper-middle-class heart for her to feel pain and loneliness.

She was a poet, and she was smoldering with subtle buried rage.

She needed redemption, and she needed it bad.

And she would start looking for romance tomorrow—after she did the next load of laundry in the six-thousand-dollar front-loading washer and dryer set Luther bought her last Mother's Day.

Luther Free
Churchman

Luther was a good husband. He just didn't like being home with his wife and three sons. He enjoyed the raucous company of jolly men— especially strong religious men who laughed loudly, played challenging board games, and relished Biblical words and phrases. Luther was morally perfect, tall, and paid his bills on time. He usually enjoyed being seen with wife Leah at important social church events. She was a "trophy," and he knew Leah violently loved his thick wallet.

He saw himself as the head of the household. His belief, surface or subconscious, was that marriage was a binding relationship whose social details were more powerful, more meaningful, than the individuals involved. He walked proudly down the sidewalk in a white shirt and tie, carrying his Bible, aloof from the sinners who had neither his cultural connections nor cash reserves.

Big Luther understood the roles. He should make money, pay bills, and have control. Leah should bake cakes, look pretty, and ask him how his day went. She should have the Scrabble boards out and dusted on schedule. And be seen but not heard.

Luther knew he was a perfect role model for his boys.

Most of the time.

But every other Friday night, Luther drove south to Santa Rey and did a little drinking—only where he knew he wouldn't be recognized. And he sometimes had lunch with the "jalapeno-hot" English professor from the community college—Katherine Van Dorn—who was stiffly intellectual but statuesque, leggy, and witty.

They were supposedly business partners of some sort.

Such escapades, of course, were unknown to his wife and three sons— and the church.

Phyllis Swiss
Adam's Wife

One month after her no-account husband Adam left her and Nebraska, Phyllis waited impatiently in a room with three wicker chairs. She had wedged herself into one chair, rather ungracefully, and looked at the old white-face analog clock, slowly ticking off increments to old age, a sagging belly, and gloomy eternity, above the exit door. She was here to see her therapist, the aged-yet-spry Dr. Kilgear. Phyllis had a strange fascination with the old man.

The last few sessions had not gone well. During their first meeting, Kilgear had told her, somewhat matter-of-factly, that she was fat, mean-spirited, and unattractive. Kilgear was from the very unpopular school of psychology—"Just Tell the Truth U." At their second encounter, he recommended she lose sixty pounds and get a better attitude. Their third meeting had been a complete disaster. She arrived wearing a mini-skirt, heels, and a lacey blouse. He had shut the door in her face and then, opening it briefly, told her to come back only if she truly wanted to change. He had shouted "Forget Victoria Secrets! You need a gym!"

Today was their last scheduled meeting. Contact would be brief. She had exciting and redemptive news for Kilgear. Yes, Phyllis had found new happiness. A fellow she'd met at karaoke night down at the Copper Queen Bar in Sutton, named Reginald, had asked her to move in with him. She couldn't wait to tell Kilgear she had been right all along. Men did love her for her good looks and sexiness.

Later in the evening, while new-squeeze Reginald was out shooting pool with his old girlfriend Buzz at the Queen, Phyllis found solace in a hot bathtub. She luxuriated in the bubbles and shaved her big thick legs, thinking about the look on old Kilgear's rough sun-damaged face when she gave him the news about Reginald. He had exclaimed, "Have you no self-respect, woman?"—and simply walked off, leaving Phyllis to settle up with the receptionist, who had quietly been filing her nails and watching *Glee* reruns on her smart phone.

Well, her therapy had cost four hundred bucks, but the counseling was well worth the expense.

Hmm. Medicaid wouldn't cover her specific therapy requirements, apparently.

She had found love again. And even though Phyllis eventually discovered Reginald had hepatitis C, she was happy and felt wanted. To further teach old Dr. Kilgear a lesson, she stopped off at the mall and bought some new lingerie. "I sure hope Reggie likes this top," she seductively whispered to herself, her breath hot and heavy, and her weighty bosom heaving with excited girlish expectations.

Lost in a happy reverie, she wondered if old man Kilgear had been with a woman within the last twenty years. She considered the romantic lives of older people, living in the trailer parks, pawing in the buffet lines, cavorting in the casinos, winking at the card games, flirting on the golf courses, whispering over at the bowling alley on 34 Highway.

Then she thought of Reginald's strong tribal-tatted arms around her, holding her tightly, teaching her to chip with a nine iron, smelling the fresh Bermuda grass in the rough, sipping an ice-cold Blitz beer, the wind blowing between her Marilyn Monroe-like legs—and she was very happy. How life had improved since Adam rode out of town. What a loser. Another educated loser—like old man Kilgear. Good riddance.

Joyfully grunting like a big bear sow, she toweled herself carefully, sprinkled fragrant powder into her many spacious and specious curves and valleys, and waited for her hard-drinking man to come home—come home to her nest of love.

The Untimely Death of Dr. Kilgear

Coincidentally, soon after Phyllis Swiss' self-removal from Dr. Kilgear's active and most-needy patient roster, the kindly and morally righteous man suffered a most tragic and bizarre accident. Somehow, an hour or so after a fairly average howling Nebraska blizzard dropped twenty-two inches of snow on the ground, the doctor was run over by his own snow blower—the mechanistic thud to Dr. Kilgear's concupiscent cranium proved fatal.

A neighbor, who nearly witnessed the accident, found the good doctor on his back, staring blankly at the low and smudged pink sun, muttering something about three weird kids with "black iris eyes" he nearly ran over with the snow blowing machine. Moments later, the doctor shouted, "Phyllis, you !@#$%" —and expired, smiling, hand over his groin.

Investigators theorized Kilgear, who went out to clear his driveway, had swerved the machine to miss an as-yet-unidentified-group of three children walking across his yard—whose footprints were found in the snow—then lost his balance and fell victim to the blower's brute force.

The funeral was held three days later. Dr. Kilgear was to be buried in his Scottish flag-emblazoned Speedo. He was once a champion channel swimmer and had still enjoyed taking laps down at the YMCA pool.

The funeral mass at the Sutton St. Stephen's Church was attended by the patients he had served and the attorneys he still owed.

Phyllis Swiss was not present.

Father Deerjohn, from San Manuel's Church over in Concho, Arizona—several states away—his connection with the deceased was somewhat mysterious—presided over the ceremony.

During the funeral, Fr. Deerjohn referred to Dr. Kilgear as a great and pious man who had carefully and thanklessly kept many souls from falling off the abrupt cliff of madness and sin.

He mentioned Kilgear's athletic ability, his tireless community service, and his great fiscal and emotional support of the local YMCA during his long and mostly stewarding life.

The crowd—many of whom were on psychiatric medication—was antsy and uncomfortable. The evening was, shall we say, disturbed and eerie—some thought they could hear the whispers of angels, or ghosts, or even children coming from outside near the atrium. The spooky Northern Lights, flashing in the late winter afternoon sky, seemed disturbed, melancholy, and perhaps even angry.

Noticing the crowd's growing discomfort and unrest, and sensing the creepy mood himself, noble Father Deerjohn ended the service with a simple prayer: "God Save Our Souls!"

The place was empty in six minutes. Father Deerjohn sprinted to his car, revved up the engine, and zoomed over to the warm and fuzzy Boogie Rheum Saloon for three quick big beers before driving back through Hamilton City and on to Concho.

The Hamilton City RV Park: A Landmark of North New Mexico

On a given winter day, about twenty-six units could be found nestled in the Hamilton City RV Park. Several were permanent or semi-permanent. Some were privately owned, but most were rentals. A few travel trailers and Class C's came and went, sure, but the population was fairly stable. It was a different story in the summer season when the travelers and tourists pulled in for a night or two. With a little ingenuity, fifty units could find access to power and a septic tank.

Park rules didn't allow for the units to be on the ground "permanently." They had to be set up like trailers or motorhomes on a camping trip. This made the park look very transient.

The park itself was old and nondescript. Spaces and power hook up boxes were on the outside of an elliptical asphalt driveway, which connected abruptly to Edison Avenue.

The elliptical driveway had speed bumps and potholes and was a source of great misery for residents and the one-man maintenance staff.

The infield contained several iconic features, including a fifties-era blue cinder block and shingled roof recreation hall and am almost-level park playground area where kids could gallop about in the summer. A single basketball hoop, the net long gone, presided over a ten by twelve cracked concrete slab. This park once had a pool, but the old swimming hole had been filled in years ago following numerous unresolvable health department issues.

A large and banged-up metal storage shed sat in the northeast corner of the infield.

Ancient toilets, trailer jacks, wheels, camper stoves, extension cords, caulk guns, pencil sharpeners, Sasquatch dolls, and paint and turpentine cans tumbled out the three-quarter closed front door. No one seemed too concerned about the mess.

In the southeast corner, an old-school laundry room with two avocado-colored washers and two white, frequently screeching, dryers gazed painfully and remorsefully at the surrounding trailers. Somehow, each laundry machine still charged only twenty-five cents a load. The building's shingled roof sagged a bit like a bad toupee. Adam Swiss spent half of his days in this room, replacing belts, vacuuming lint, emptying change, and unclogging drains.

A "Teem" pop machine, faded and dented, stood guard just outside the un-lockable front door. But it wasn't plugged in.

Mr. Evans, the park manager, resided with his comely and obedient wife at the front of the park, just off Edison, in a robust-appearing polished Airstream which currently sported a green holiday wreath and a red bow. As park CEO and CFO, he made arrangements with overnight guests, collected rent money from the lifers, and oversaw maintenance. He would rather be elk hunting or ice fishing.

He had learned to tolerate his enchanting wife of fifty-one years. She put up with him too.

Tall and straight, with frosted and helped-along blonde hair (and a firm buttocks structure), Mrs. Evans still had a twinkle in her eye and a wiggle in her walk.

Mrs. Evans had many friends in the RV Park. But she did not like the Widow Douglas. She liked Chip the Bug Man, though. Yes. Very much.

Often, lovely old Mrs. Evans watched the handy man Adam Swiss at work, especially when he was nearby and bent over, fixing a water pipe or faucet.

Sometimes, while keeping an eye on the handy man, she twirled a strand of frosted hair, licked her freshly-glossed lips and teeth, and flexed her toes, murmuring pleasant interjections to herself and smiling at the throbbing world.

Sure seemed like there were always big "fix-it" problems with a rental or something down at the Recreation Hall or laundry room. Yep, plenty of troubles to keep a handy man busy in the RV Park.

Sol Davies Considers Love
in the Hamilton RV Park

Old Man Davies was a long term "alpha" resident in the RV Park. His wife had left him many years ago because of his sloth and drinking and his fixation with watching insignificant winter sports like curling on cable TV year round.

Yes, Old Sol looked bad now, but he still had creative energy.

He periodically wondered how much loving was going on among his neighbors. His friend, Chad Duhbu, told him once, "Chicks are everywhere! The good thing about being eighty-two is that seventy-year-old dames still look good to me!"

Sol had never been much of a lover. He had fathered seven children. None of them were in touch with him anymore and three were in prison, but it all seemed sort of matter-of-fact or scripted to him. In the back of his mind was some strange notion about continuing the family tree, the Davies bloodline.

If the truth were known—he had never bought his wife flowers, jewelry, candy, a birthday card, or even talked to her other than to ask about supper or demand a beer.

Curiously, he wondered why people worked all their lives and raised kids then sold all their junk and moved into RV parks. Fulfilled, they swapped lies and wives and liquor and seemed to have a good time. The world appeared so backward to Sol, although each beer he drank brought him closer to some crystal-clear awareness about how things should be.

He noticed a rich blue green fungus growing under his toenail, then took a deep swallow of golden beer to get him refocused on the problems at hand. And there were many, so many.

Nowadays, people talked about date night and anniversary cruises and Girls Night Out and all of the silly, corporate, expensive programmed stuff. What happened to the good old days when a man worked, the wife cooked, and there was no trouble? Work all week, mow the lawn Saturday, grill Saturday evening in the summer, church early Sunday whether you needed it or not, then the Yankees on TV in the afternoon.

What more was there?

"H——," said Sol, still looking at his toenail. "There have been a lot of changes in my life, and I've been against most every one of 'em."

Sol figured about nineteen couples lived in the RV Park, along with several singles. He thought only the Widow Douglas still had her looks. Most of the men had big bellies, bald heads, and hearing aids. They wore suspenders and belts at the same time to hold up their trousers. A few sported bad looking gold chain necklaces and most sucked in their big guts when younger women came to visit the park. Their faces had become rounded, almost baby-like. In the summer, the old boys all wore the same kind of sandals with socks.

The old boys' wives looked like nineteenth century grandmas and chatted endlessly about recipes, buffet lines, and their former work lives.

He noticed lately a few of the old gals had new blue-ink "tramp stamp" tattoos and tribal art stenciled over their varicose veins. Ugh.

The tattoos made him shiver with nausea, but he still looked anyway.

In the winter, a few "senior" residents headed south to Arizona or New Mexico.

"Good riddance," said Sol out loud. "And take your d—— shuffleboard with you!"

But Sol heard rumors about the hard-drinking parties, the love triangles, the swaps, and the good-time loving late at night. Oh, yes, there were little pathways, little trails, worn through the lawns to the back doors and patios where the hammocks waited patiently, empty but hopeful.

Sol found wrinkly old women unattractive—even after seven or twenty beers. He was skeptical of senior swinging stories, but...

It had been a long time for old Sol. Life had pretty much passed him by. Even so, he still relished a good cold beer and a hockey game.

Sol kept his eyes wide open, behind sunglasses, of course, so no one could tell.

Well. Not much got past Sol, even when sober.

He noticed one bug exterminator spent a lot of time over at the Widow Douglas' doublewide—and at the park manager's shiny trailer up front. A lot of time.

That exterminator, Chip, always had a silly grin on his face.

The Bug Man and his smelly, bobbing, chemical wand visited the Widow about twice a week.

Hmm, thought Sol, she must have one h—— of a big cockroach problem.

The Widow, at sixty-one, always smelled good and was very curvy. Her skin looked like recently-tanned leather in some places, but still, she could attract a second glance even from younger fellows. She maintained the strut, and the wiggle, and reminded old Sol of Ann-Margaret. Sol liked to believe he himself still looked like Dean Martin, especially Dean Martin in cowboy movies. But he actually looked more like Don Rickles.

Sometimes Sol wondered what happened to his face. When he examined himself in the mirror, Sol saw a big, round, and furtive baby face looking back at him. Angles and the characteristics of youth were gone, relegated to black and white photos stuck in a scrapbook somewhere.

Yes, he was on the decline now, but his social security check paid the rent, cable, and brought him beer.

The hell with women, he thought, as he watched Bug Man Chip nonchalantly squeezing the Widow's hindquarters as he came out her small back door—waving his long brass wand in the late morning air.

Sol, with more vocal power, said out loud to himself, "The hell with women," and cracked open another good cold beer—probably his BFF. He picked up today's *Hamilton Democrat* newspaper and slowly read some crazy article about recent local sightings of hybrid alien-human children with black eyes. "Are these people nuts?" he asked out loud. And then he dozed off, thinking about following a hammock trail or two to see what he could find.

Jeanine Douglas
Widow

Each Thursday at about noon, Mrs. Douglas drove her sunburned old Corolla down to the Great Northeastern Super Chinese Buffet. A widow now for seven years, and relatively young, she enjoyed "getting out" to the buffet for sushi and lo mien. Sometimes she went with a group of ladies from The Park—often she enjoyed sitting by herself, slurping big noodles, and people watching, while attractive, firm, young male Chinese workers kept the food lines moving.

Mrs. Douglas kept her appearance neat and trimmed. Childless—she had discovered only late in her marriage her husband was gay and infertile—she still had a girlish figure and terrific legs. Jeanine knew there were many rumors about her movements around the RV Park. Her relationship with Chip the Exterminator was obvious—she had no regrets about her occasional "meetings" with the firm and muscular young man who drove the rusted, rumbling pickup.

Certainly, she sensed she was one of Chip's playthings. But what did it matter? The Widow still had desire, and Chip was handy, willing, and able, which was more than she could say for most of the old pot-bellied boozing duffers living in the Park.

The Widow loved sushi—and she enjoyed hot spicy soup. As already mentioned, she usually came to the buffet alone, but on one occasion, she and Chip met her for lunch. She remembered feeding him won tons with a spoon until he was so aroused they had to whisk away to the parking lot for dessert. Yum.

Mrs. Douglas was one of those sixty-year-old gals who still looked sparklingly good in lingerie. She had the legs going, most certainly.

Oh, the Widow attended church and played canasta on Wednesday afternoons down at the Lodge, and worked for several charitable organizations. Still, she longed for the good life she never had.

Her circle of friends had grown smaller as her dalliances with Chip became more frequent and public. The old gals in the Park loved to talk about the Widow.

Jeanine heard whispers daily about "vulgarity" and "she could be his mother" and "she has no shame."

Old Lady Evans, the park manager's homely, rough-looking wife, was always giving the Widow the "evil" eye. Sometimes they'd meet at the row of beat-up tin mailboxes which served the sustainable postal needs of "permanent" Park residents—their icy glares could freeze Phoenix in July.

But, at a curvy 61, how many more chances would the Widow Douglas get? And Chip had a way about him, yes indeed. And his long brass wand? Well....

Arnie, the Moonbucks Barista, Catches His Mom with the Bug Man:
A Quirky but Meaningful Episode Occurring Just Blocks Away from the RV Park

Arnie worked part time as a Barista at Moonbucks. He knew a great deal about sustainability, voter registration issues, wealth redistribution, animal rights, whip cream, Wi-Fi, and lattes. He still lived at home with his folks, even though he was thirty-two. Because he didn't have much money, the young man rode a fazer scooter to work. Most days.

Sometimes he caught a ride with his mom or one of the other Baristas. His preference was Sandi Tea—she was volcano hot! At least that's what the other male baristas said. Sometimes Arnie thought she smelled funny. Sometimes he was very uncomfortable around girls. Arnie was having trouble finding himself, but he found it pretty easy to stay at home, to live in the basement and play video games in his spare time.

His mother was a vibrant, bouncy, saucy redhead of fifty-three, still quite attractive and slim.

One day, Arnie came home from work early and caught his mom making out with the bug exterminator in the back yard. Arnie was taken back at first, but seeing his mom enjoying sweaty, vigorous, physical contact with a stranger was deliciously charming for the entrenched and doomed youth.

He watched them kissing, groping, and nuzzling out there under the snow dripping cedars. Though he would never admit to being a voyeur, or emotionally sick, Arnie felt himself enthralled, captivated, even possessed by this powerful, near mythic, image.

The exterminator wasn't much older than Arnie.

Physical labor had been kind to Chip. He had nicely formed arms and his chest muscles rippled—his name patch-emblazoned shirt was unbuttoned at the throat clear down to his navel, even in the chilly late fall air. His hairy, chemical-soaked upper body was heaving and steaming with desire. Chip was a stallion, a raging boar, a man among men, a Trojan for sure.

Arnie could see Chip was wearing a wedding band on his right middle finger. Hard to tell what that meant.

Then his mom was standing on her toes, kissing the Bug Man, Chip, with great passion. Arnie had never seen such a lip lock. This unholy couple groaned in machined, beveled unison. Birds and squirrels in the trees and rabbits on the brownish grey lawn stopped to watch the terrible twosome's titanic, titillating, torrid tango. Their breath, hot and moist, clouded up this portion of the shadowed back yard.

Suddenly, his dad pulled into the driveway, pushing the BOW's nose up to the edge of the portioning shrubs demarcating the back yard from the insidious and sinful grove.

Animals and birds, screeching and chattering their disapproval, disappeared into the frost-damaged brush. Even the icicles seemed chiding.

The couple sprung apart like they were on springs. Mom tore tufts of glistening hair from Chip's turgid flesh. He grimaced but then smiled, coyly.

Close call, Arnie thought. But his fat old man never saw a thing.

Beating a quick retreat, nimble Chip was in his company truck, the one with big floppy bug antennae, and gone. Wait, no, he came back, asking for a signature on the work order from Dad.

Satisfied the deal was complete, and lighting up a smoke, Chip drove away slowly and with swagger, although he seemed to have a certain strained and pained look in his eyes. Big Earl, Pre-Owned BOW Automotive Sales Specialist, and Arnie's biological dad, mopped his sweaty face with a handkerchief, hitched up his lime-green stretchy pants, and ambled into the house, looking for a Blitz beer.

Arnie's mom stood squinting into the setting pink sun, pulling her sweater closer, watching Chip's rumbling truck vanish down the street. Sighing, she straightened her blouse, wiped her mouth with a hanky, sniffed sadly, and returned to domestic life. The BOW tinkled as she walked by.

This high life moment had passed.

Chip was gone.

Arnie felt a twinge of sadness for her. He watched the truck drive away too.

Still thinking of Chip and his firm, ripped, and hairy torso, Arnie went in the house and joined his dad for a good cold beer. Ah. Yum. Snap.

Willie G
Living Mannequin

Young Willie Garrison had a most interesting job. He worked as a living mannequin in the front window at The Espressions Clothing Boutique. Each day he wore different clothes and periodically assumed different poses and postures as the happy shopping population of his city walked by. Sometimes he wore seasonal garments, like a tight-fitting Speedo or a bulky polar bear parka. But usually he wore a variety of polo shirts, or slacks, or sweaters, or nice combos, especially during the back-to-school season.

Willie came to this job rather unexpectedly. He had been a receptionist at the Go Green Power Plant, but his supervisor, Luther, had fired him for telling inappropriate lewd jokes on the job site. Willie held no bitterness towards Luther, but he missed the good, government subsidized salary he had been earning in the solar industry.

Willie once saw Luther giggling and hugging one of the male custodians out on the back loading ramp of the plant, but he said nothing. What was there to say?

Sometimes he wondered if Luther saw him in the shadows,

peeking around the corner, with a clammy hand over his wicked smile. Oh well. So it went. Hmm.

Willie now made ten dollars an hour, striking provocative and interesting poses while lame techno-music blared in the background. He earned about $300 a week pretending to be "engaged" with fashion and apparel. Acting was a pretty good gig.

On better days, he considered himself to be a dramatic player. Yes.

Sometimes he felt like Red Skelton doing a clown skit. Sometimes, when he was wearing a pirate outfit or something sea-worthy similar, he saw himself as Johnny Depp.

When he wore a vampire costume, he noticed crowds of women gathering in front of the store, panting, staring, giggling, and clapping their hands.

He often wondered about his city's fascination with vampires, wizards, the walking dead, she-wolves, Sasquatches, shape-shifters, and coffee shops. Didn't anybody have a life?

Willie was not the brightest bulb in the box, but this new job made him very philosophical. He had come to recognize he had always been a living mannequin; always in a store window watching life pass by, watching the happy couples strolling arm in arm, kissing in the moonlight, stealing a squeeze, a quick grab, between the, uh, between the traffic light changes.

Willie knew everyone in town, almost, and sensed he was an outsider even though he had lived here his entire life. He saw so many beautiful women walking by, usually holding hands with creepy-looking dudes and losers. His ongoing observation provided him with an unsolvable riddle: Why did it seem good looking, pleasant women always got involved with windbags, pretenders, posers, and eventual failures?

Willie has had few dates in his life. Oh, he looked OK, but his oddness betrayed him. Too, since leaving Go Green, his personal economy had been diminished.

He had taken a few girls out for pizza and good conversation. Things never worked romantically for Willie. The ladies always wanted more than pizza and polite behavior. He never had a second date with any girl. One leggy and tasty brunette named Allyson told him, rather directly, after he stole a kiss and hug from her—and she didn't like it! — "Willie, your wallet is too small. How can you show a girl a good time without any money?"

Willie enjoyed being a mannequin.

He could glare and grimace at the pretty girls when they walked by Espressions and pointed and laughed at him. Surely he had made the right career move.

Someday, though, he knew he would like to be a novelist—and write a story about his mannequin man experiences....

Joey (Joe) Smith

Joey Smith lived in a nice park model trailer that was still on wheels within Hamilton City RV Park. He resided just across from the laundry mat, which was handy. Joey was twenty-three years old. He had lived in this park model since he left his parents' home back in the summer of 2007—right after finishing high school with a C average.

Joey worked at Jann's IBC Super Mart grocery store. He started working at Jann's part time when he was fourteen. Back in those days, he was a bagger and on-call cart collector. He also shoveled snow off the parking lot in winter and took apart cardboard boxes for recycling. Nowadays, he worked as the second shift floor manager, and had responsibility for keeping the shelves stocked and faced properly. He supervised a staff of three—young kids just starting out, much like he did so many years ago.

Joey didn't like being called Joey around the store anymore, so we have decided to call him Joe.

Joe made a pretty good living down at Jann's IBC. With overtime, he grossed around 35K a year. This was more than enough to make the $159 a month payment on his park model and the $250 a month rent on his trailer space.

He bought a $50 face value I bond each month for the future. He didn't own a car, though, and still rode the same mountain bike with a chrome bell he had in high school. He wanted to take the bell off, but the clamp was rusted onto the handle bar. Joe was a hard worker. He enjoyed squirrel hunting and fishing and reading western novels.

Joe didn't care a good !@#$% hoot about wealth redistribution or how much his boss made. He just wanted to pay his bills and be self-sufficient. Crazy.

Joe visited his parents often, but was careful not to "hang around" his folks' place too much. He was a man now and had his own life and concerns.

Joe had a live-in girlfriend named Star. She had a very pretty face. Star weighed four-hundred-fifty-pounds. But Joe didn't notice her weight. She was a good friend, a great lover, and provided ongoing support for his personal and career aspirations.

Star knew how to wear the right kind of eye shadow and lip gloss, and her "secret" scent was, well, demonic. She could rev up Joe's engines like, well, like a nitro-methane dragster. Star knew how to be a natural woman for Joe. Wow! Her size meant nothing to him—her heart was a galaxy of repose and comfort for Joe. Yes, this mattered.

Sometimes, when they were finished loving, the couple smoked unfiltered cigarettes and talked about the future. Star worked at the Olden Country Corner Endless Buffet as a taste tester. Quality control, you know, mandated by OCCEB's Operational Plan! But she had strategically targeted the personal goal to become a cashier within a year—and hopefully double her pay. She was excited about Joe's career prospects. She hoped they would be able to buy a new single wide, or maybe a good used doublewide, within a year. Their park model was simply too small for her.

Just last week, enjoying the Christmas season, they walked hand-in-hand, smooching, and wandered down Hamilton City's streets. For all they knew, they were in Paris or Moscow or Madrid in April. They walked in a fragrance of blossoms even though it was frosty December, and their laughter tinkled upward to an honest and appreciative heaven. For such was love.

Certainly a man appreciated a little support for his endeavors… Just a little.

Dandy Dan
The Ice Cream Man

Daniel Smith had given up his job as math division secretary over at Copperfield Community College to start his own business. He now owned The Rock and Rollin' Ice Cream Truck—and drove up and down Hamilton City's streets to sell confectionary treats. He typically had Van Halen's "Ice Cream Man" blasting away from the six subwoofers mounted on top of his 1974 converted Econoline van.

Business was pretty good, and he hoped the frozen confectionary industry might pay the rent until he could get his musical career up and running.

He actually paid no rent. More below.

Later today, Dan was going to hand letter The Rock and Rollin' Mission Statement and Strategic Vision on the starboard side of his van—for such was business now. He would most certainly fail if his stakeholders did not know about his mission and vision. Yes.

Dan played bass guitar. His technique was a little sloppy, he used a pick, but he was good at playing root five country music and could quarter note his way through most rock songs. He knew some musician types, including Bob Zontarg, a hard rockin' janitor over at the college, and a sound guy named AV Allen.

Dan was mostly interested in writing original songs, but he had trouble finding enough time to practice or put a "real" band together.

Dan was thirty-six years old now. Life had been pretty good to him. He lived in a travel trailer parked in his parents' driveway. His mom did his laundry for him twice a week.

Dan was very good at playing paint ball and laser tag. Many of his closest friends were in junior high. He no longer had an iPhone because he couldn't afford the monthly service fee. Dan's dad let him park his ice cream truck next to the travel trailer. The HOA hadn't complained yet, but it was probably only a matter of time.

Dan needed to read the HOA's Mission and Values Statement.

Dan was concerned global warming might harm his ice cream business. He hoped to save up enough money to buy a hybrid power ice cream truck someday. But such a purchase was probably far into his future. Plus, the recent increasingly cold winters have caused him to become obtusely cynical about the media's ongoing portrayal of climate change. Go figure.

Dan practiced his bass after work. He always closed the windows in his travel trailer before he plugged his Chinese bass into a ten watt Chinese practice amplifier. He hoped he would be able to pick up a few dollars playing at the local Moonbucks. Dan realized it was very hard to be a solo bass act. But he didn't know yet that Moonbucks wouldn't pay him a nickel. They might give him a cup of coffee. Maybe.

Dan needed to read the Moonbucks' Mission and Values Statement.

With next week's earnings, Dan was going to get his lip pierced. He believed this cosmetic alteration might help him find a girlfriend and make him a better musician.

Dan wanted to be a "Ladies' Man." Yes. Mr. Bass Player had his eye on a gal who worked at the convenience mart over on Edison. "She's a looker," he said out loud to himself each time he drove past the mart, subwoofers blasting away, visions of big-hair bands dancing before him, fame just a death metal-imitating song or two away.

Shadows on the Sun
The RV Park Couple No One Has Met [Yet]

Tennessee Williams knew distinctly
—No shadows dance upon the Sun
And now you know it, too
But the sun shines anyway...
Yes, the pair lives together in an older single wide
A two-room palace smelling like ash trays, old coffee, and
      ecumenical paint.
He might have looked like Elvis (the 50's Elvis) three decades
      ago…
She is still a beauty, hardened some. Though her tattoos have lost
      that etched
and sexy look, she still turns heads... and has a poignant "way"
      any male or
female might recognize.
Yes,   they   still   cut impressive   figures together—but
      anachronistic—
Sometime, long ago, they left Public lives together

and rode a bus to Hamilton City, and thought they'd stay a day or
two—walking
hand-in-hand through the diesel fumes, neither excited nor
dismayed. Some time went by—
Then they waited to see if spouses were angry or perplexed—
They never heard a thing from the Old World—now, in late
middle age,
Still they live and love in a rent-by-the-week mobile home,
Bathed in eerie and accusing pink light each winter morning—
Haunted by frosty windows in the dark sky December…
They wander to the Blue Caboose Diner for most meals
Coupling down cracked and slippery concrete sidewalks
Without cares but with many cares…
He listens to the world on an old AM transistor radio
She reads newspapers someone left behind—
and paints her nails and adjusts toe rings each morning …
He shaves a weathered face carefully, with a blade and mug of
manly lather—
The modern age, the spiritus mundi, well that means nothing to
this dyad. They have each other…
Sure, they live and love in a rented mobile
They love with the freshness of just-cut Timothy Hay, of
Morning Glories, and the late April Rain…
There are no shadows dancing on the Sun…
But the sun shines anyway …

Frank Eastermann

Well, Frank was a colorful character. Many years ago, he had been a factory motorcycle road racer—he had rides with Yamaha and Ducati. After fracturing his legs and arms a few times during one-hundred-mph Gary Nixon-chasing crashes at Talladega and Daytona back in his twenties, he took up motorcycle mechanics at a local bike shop until landing a very nice small engine repair teaching gig at Copperfield Community College. Now, at sixty-five, he was retired and living quietly in his paid-for small motor home.

Now Mr. Eastermann suffered from a bizarre kind of anxiety or emotional problem. He could not bear the sight of beautiful women. Frank had no success with girls back when he was in high school but did find brief happiness with one of his racetrack groupies in the late seventies. Curvy, bodacious, and sculpted, Wanda stayed with him as long as he was garnishing podium spots. But after femur-shattering wreck number three, she left him for an Isle of Man TT champion.

Forty or so later, Frank still awoke some nights in a sweat, in a panic, painfully remembering he had only known some kind of intimacy with a female for one hundred twenty-six days of his life, now

23,825 days long and counting.

Oh, at his age he should let it go. Of course! His romantic journey was nearly over now. But he still frequently reverted to bad reflections, counterproductive musings. All those years without companionship. No family. No romance, no perfumed aroma on the pillow, no high heels akimbo on the bedroom floor, no one asking about his day. No dates, dances, dinners, or cooing on the patio or between the sheets. Nope, no late night loving in the cookies and cream fragranced candlelight after a few salty margaritas at Bike Night down on the town square. Nope. Nada.

He could not bear to watch television. Too many beautiful girls. He never went to the movies. Ah, the romances around him—real and pretend—always beat him down. He could not read motorcycle magazines—too many ads with perfect-looking umbrella girls and parts models in miniskirts. Legs, delicious legs, everywhere! Country music, rock music, opera—ah, no music for Frank. Certainly not the Blues. OMG! Too much material reminded him of his bleak life.

For a time, Frank did enjoy listening and grooving to the three-piece Moondoggs band down at Moonbucks. Just too much lovin' in rockabilly.

So, that became insufferable, also. He was Roderick Usher of the modern age.

Where had he gone wrong? What had he done to deserve this abject loneliness?

Much of his situation was his own fault, of course. He had seldom attended staff parties, or gone to church, or been involved socially at any level with anybody. He had a few friends at the college still, but once you retired, well, that was pretty much it. You didn't get invited to potlucks or birthday parties anymore.

No Potlucks, no parties.

For quite a long time, he worked on the idea all women wanted a man with a big wallet—or men who were red-hot lovers—or romantic girly men who could cook or who always brought flowers. Going on a cruise—or staying at a "cute" bed and breakfast—or joining a gym? Ah, the women loved all that. None of it suited Frank, though. He was what we thought he was.

To the Here and Now!

This afternoon, Frank drove his car to the convenience store and bought a twelve pack of good cold Blitz beer. Charmain, the hot, big-bosomed red-headed, always-friendly, forty-year-old clerk, held her hand out for his $13.40. He did not look her in the eyes. He had to get home as quickly as possible. Collecting his change, then hastily going through the door, he bumped into a sweet-smelling woman, with great looking ankles, wearing a silver crucifix. Her image—beautiful, poised, and even forgiving—nearly made him ill. He sprinted across the parking lot, hurled himself into the Toyota, and closed his eyes. The former professor gripped the steering wheel until his knuckles were white and cramped, not knowing what to do, not knowing where to go. But then Frank remembered he still had a good cold twelve pack sitting beside him—his BFF. And he felt better.

Charmain, strangely confused for an instant, wished she had learned his name. What a cute old guy, she thought to herself. Wish he'd ask me over for a beer.

Johnny Roz
Retired English Teacher

Now, Johnny's one claim to fame was that he had graded over 430,000 essays during his twenty-five year teaching career at Copperfield Community College. Johnny was an old bachelor. He lived in a nice two-tone pink and silver travel trailer owned by Luther and Leah Free. Johnny had lived there for nineteen years and had never considered home ownership. His days were spent worrying about faucet leaks, laundry, paying bills, and doctors' appointments. Johnny's cousin was Dr. Jeffrey Roz, a somewhat formerly-famous poet, romance novelist, and scholar who taught at nearby Hamilton State University.

Johnny's story was pretty calm. He couldn't tell you where the years went. He was young once, went to a few meetings, then he was fifty-three and eligible for the state retirement system. He had owned three or four dogs in his lifetime, a few used cars, and might have been to Saskatoon once. That's it. Except for the time he nearly killed himself drinking tequila shots at a CCC staff Christmas party in Casita Grande. The next morning, he woke up covered in sleet on somebody's patio, pants gone, nearly hypothermic.

Johnny was a capable and careful man who kept a clean apartment. He wasn't hooked up to cable, or dish TV, but he occasionally watched network events on the seven inch screen antenna-driven handheld model he bought at Sticky Mart for forty bucks.

Johnny had never been married. He often wondered about the life he lived, and realized financial security provided little in the way of emotional comfort.

Johnny had always been fascinated by women, but had realized few "connections" with them. He had maintained female friends at work, but not many. Women, to Johnny, seemed to represent some kind of problem—a beautiful yet complicated problem.

A bit of a rhetorician, he often spent his days contemplating, analyzing, and critically reviewing the following question relating to human behavior: What do women want? Ah, Johnny knew Chaucer had an answer, Jerry Springer was curious, Virginia Woolf had a speculative idea or thirty, and Hollywood had churned out their notions in millions of senses-numbing bad movies, but he himself was at a total loss. Since he didn't know the answer, Johnny often surmised he would remain lonely and solitary. Snap.

Sometimes he woke up at night sweating, nearly panicked, and thought about his past and the emptiness of his meager experiences.

John was having a series of dreams lately—those kinds you have in the moments before you wake up—which were totally depressing him. In the dreams, the formula, the plot line, was nearly always the same. To wit:

Julia, an attractive and unhappily-married housewife from down the street, knocks on his door. He opens the door to see her, smiling, holding a measuring cup in her left hand. In each of the dreams, she has

44

asked for something different—sometimes sugar, sometimes milk, sometimes cream, sometimes salsa, sometimes peanut oil. Once she even asked for cloves of garlic. He invites her into the front room, takes the cup, and finds the spice or ingredient she needs back in the kitchen. When he returns to the darkening room, she is always sitting on the couch, twirling a strand of auburn hair with one hand, and, with the other, patting the couch, signaling him to sit down next to her, next to her shapely form.

Her lips are pouty and beyond energized. She breathes heavily, with poignant and powerful desire. Her legs cross and uncross rhythmically. Um. Can you feel the heat?

Johnny always places the cup on his beat-up old coffee table and looks into Julia's clear eyes—crystal pools of composure and need.

She puts her arms around him and nuzzles his chicken-skin wrinkly neck, and then she snuggles into Johnny. Now her lips are moist and panting. The old guy reaches out and hugs her, feels her curves, and is overwhelmed by a gloaming sense of comfort, love, connection. Her breath is sweet, her hands are satin, and the moment is warm and complete. One might say his senses are satiated, short circuited, nurtured, mesmerized, and radicalized. In other words, he is turned on but in a very private, emotionally pure, and enriched manner.

He smells her grace and beauty. Her grey eyes look into his for just a moment, and he can see into eternity—blazing, abrupt, and terrifying. The smart phones are silent; the music is quiet. Only her pulsating and harmonic breathing remains. The aroma of the eternal, the archetypical perfect female drifts into his nostrils. His being becomes an integrated whole—unified and sanctified. She murmurs pleasantries, licks his left ear lobe, then stands up, straightens her straps, and leaves, thanking him for the cupful. He admires her tight jeans, her straight hair, and her long neck as she leaves the room.

But the dream is always pure and potent and always the same. And comet quick! The sequence takes about thirty seconds, probably. This is the most love Johnny has ever felt.

And he wakes up tired, turns on the calcium-corroded coffee pot, and lurches into another lonely day.

Sometimes when Johnny was outside, he would see Julia coming down the street, perhaps walking the dog, or jogging, or visiting a friend. At such times, old Johnny turned away; he could not bear to see her curves, straight hair, and grey eyes. How much eternity could a man take?

Truth was Julia wasn't married. Oddly enough, she often thought of old Roz and wondered about his life, his style, his weltanschauung. Crazy. She was miserable, too.

Leah's Random Meeting with Adam

Back to the story. So, on one murky, misty, and drizzly early December Monday morning, Adam Swiss had been knee deep in a septic tank pumping job in the RV Park. He and Gus, the guy from Hamilton City Go Green Waste Removal, were finishing up the project. Gus, who had the better gloves on, was coiling up the flexible hose on the back of the truck. Adam noticed a familiar-looking Lexus coming to a halt along Edison Avenue about twenty-five yards away from where he stood. When the car stopped, an attractive woman, also vaguely familiar, got out of the car and walked to the driver's side rear. Apparently, the tire had gone flat.

"You got this, Gus?" Swiss asked the waste technician while gazing at the big wheeled Lexus.

In the back ground, P.O.D's "Boom" was blasting away on Adam's docked iPod. Now that might have been portentous!

"Sure, Swiss. Thanks for helping. We have an open PO with the park so you don't need to sign nothin.' I'll take this big load of stinky hot sh— down to the station. See ya later. D——. Look at the gal over by the Lexus! Man is she hot!"

The poor guy's jaw had dropped to his brown-stained knees.

But Swiss hadn't heard any of the last part of Gus' observations. He was closing fast on the Lexus and Mrs. Free.

As he approached, clumping along in his big rubber galoshes, she looked up, cautiously. The guy approaching her, though bald-head and sort of gangly—still looked oddly charming. He was attractive in a rough-cut, blue-collar kind of way.

"Hi," said Adam. "Looks like you have a flat."

"Yes," she replied. "But I'm okay. Sort of. I was going to call Triple D, but it turns out my phone battery is dead."

Adam, peering under the rear of the Lexus, saw the spare tire was in good shape and inflated. "Do you have a jack?"

"I think so. It's in this compartment back here in the floor board. I guess. I don't know much about cars. I don't know how to jack it up. "

Adam found the jack and the handle and a lug wrench. A few minutes later, the tires were switched, and she was ready to go. But she hesitated. "Look, uh, my name is Leah Free. I so appreciate your help." Trying to conjure up something appropriate as payment for this smelly but charming dude's kindness, she blurted out, "Can I buy you lunch for helping me?"

"Well, you don't have to do all that," replied Adam, "but sure, I'd like to have lunch with you. I really, really need to clean up first, though."

"Okay, fine, uh, do you want to meet down at Mymy's Café at noon?"

"Wow," said Adam. "I'll see you down there. I usually take my lunch break about then. Mymy's sounds terrific."

He was thinking to himself, *Are you bringing those legs?*

She felt a passionate inclination to hug him or shake his hand or kiss his cheek or something, but thought better. Sweet as he was, he smelled horrific. Leah moved into her urban super-chariot smoothly and drove off, waving and smiling graciously.

Adam waved and headed over to his trailer for a cleaning. Gus was still rolling up his long hose.

After a ten minute scrubbing in his two x two fiberglass shower stall with the pot metal showerhead, Swiss put on his good jeans and flannel shirt and rolled out the Yamaha DT-1. He headed out to Mymy's wondering what this all meant.

Why do men always wonder what events represent when they may

actually mean nothing?

Lunch with the Luscious Lassie, Mrs. Free
12:10 PM on Monday

Adam became reacquainted with Leah about forty-nine minutes after she drove her Big Wheel Lexus down Edison Avenue. She was seated, cross-legged, properly, at a table for two on the patio at Mymy's. He wondered if she knew he rode in on a motorcycle (She did, actually, and was quite pleased.) Always ravishing, Leah looked strangely refreshed, even though Swiss knew she could not possible have gone home to shower and fix her hair. Ah, so many mysteries about females remain unsolved, unresolved.

"Hello, Leah. Thank you for inviting me down to lunch. I'm not sure I've actually eaten here. A Big Red burger at McDougal's is probably my big lunch out. This is quite a charming venue."

"You are certainly welcome, Mr. Swiss. It's the least I could do. I suppose my husband might have come along eventually, but he isn't very mechanically inclined anyway. And he is always quite busy with business and financial matters. I'm sure he would have called someone. I am very happy to meet you. I believe I have heard you play guitar and sing down at Moonbucks."

At that exact moment, husband Luther Free walked into Mymy's Café with Dr. Kat Van Dorn. The tall red-headed English professor was a bit tipsy, even though it was barely noon. She held tightly to Luther's arm and was walking "into" him, not beside him. Giggling. Her lipstick was blurred, and a smudge still highlighted Luther's left ear.

Luther, spotting his wife, and not really seeing Adam, began stuttering and sputtering. "Uh, hi, Leah, this is uh, ah, a business associate, Katherine, honey, from the college. She is interested in our apartment building over on Allworthy Street."

A "potted" yet pitiful and perfectly pretty Prof. Van Dorn extended her left hand as Leah Free rose—like a Big Bad Genie—out of her chair.

What happened next became part of Hamilton City and Copperfield Community College mythic lore.

Dr. Van Dorn never saw it coming. Leah Free, eyes ablaze, drove her right fist into Van Dorn's face, and her left into the professor's upper midsection.

Wham! Bam! Stars! Oomph! Crack! Lightning Bolt! A jab and another jab!

Knocked cold, Kat, newly catatonic, cascaded and crumpled towards the concrete floor, then was carefully caught and caressed by a startled Luther, church bulletin in his back pocket.

Adam, stunned by the events, heard Leah Free's voice. "Get me out of here, Swiss."

Then, staring at the pummeled, peppered, semi-prone Van Dorn, Leah shouted, "And I never liked you as a teacher, either!"

Luther was hollering at the gathering crowd, "For God's sake, get some ice and a glass of water! She's coming around."

The prim and proper packaged potluck patrons on the patio panicked.

So much for lunch en plein air.

Thoughtful, Swiss queried out loud, "Should I leave a tip?"

The uncomfortable restaurant patrons, anxious for some kind of polite relief, roared with laughter.

The town's newest couple hopped on the DT-1 and rattled down the street, the old two-stroker motorcycle smoking like a mosquito fogger.

"Where to?" asked Swiss. Leah shouted into his ear, "Any place, your place, please get me away from here. I think I'm gonna be sick."

And she was!

Ding, Ding. Round One was over.

Copperfield Community College Parking Lot
8:40 AM on Tuesday, Finals Week

A sore but unrepentant Dr. Van Dorn exited her car and was heading towards the Language and Lit building at Copperfield Community College. As she crossed the drive, she heard footsteps behind her. "Dr. Van Dorn, can you give me a minute?" Relieved to hear a man's voice, she turned to meet the approaching Dr. Preston. His crystal earring glistened in the sun. His shoes were immaculate.

"Ah, yes, Dean Preston," she said, looking down, trying to avoid direct eye contact with the scrutinizing administrator. "Good morning, ah, yes. How may I help you? I must get to my nine am class directly."

The ubiquitous Dean, who enjoyed Dr. Van Dorn's legs but not her seething intellect, replied in a charming voice, "And good morning to you, Katherine. I simply wanted to let you know President Dolly will be contacting you this morning—something about a brawl involving college staff at a downtown restaurant or pub yesterday. My, your face seems quite bruised. Did you have an accident at home? Trip over a vacuum cleaner? You should probably get your eye looked at."

Smugly, he turned and walked away, suddenly waving joyfully to

Counselor Vasquez, also walking through the parking lot.

Prof. Van Dorn's ribs hurt, her face hurt. And now the college president wanted to see her.

Great, she thought to herself. But at least I'm gonna end up with my man Luther. And nobody's ever gonna beat us at Scrabble.

Not wanting to face the day, she texted the division secretary and asked her to notify students that class was cancelled till Thursday. She got back in her car and headed down to the Copper Coin for a bloody Mary. Then she left a cryptic message on Luther's phone: *L'amour fait les plus grandes douceurs et les plus sensibles infortunes de la vie*— *from* Madeleine de Scudéry.

For those of you who aren't global corporate citizens or who can't read French just yet, the translation follows: *Love is responsible for the greatest pleasures and the worst problems in life.*

Kat Van Dorn's Townhome
8:15 PM

Kat and Luther were snuggling on her couch. They were gently playing a game of Scrabble—Roman Rumble Rampage Rules. She had an ice pack on her right eye and a martini in her left hand. Luther, temporarily distracted from the Scrabble board, was kissing her long and inviting neck. His fleshy hands rested gently on her mounds of joy.

"Baby," he said, breathing heavily to Dr. Van Dorn. "I talked to my lawyer and she says we should file charges, assault charges, against lascivious lunatic Leah. We can have her arrested. She had no right to do this."

"Luther," croaked cute, kittenish, curvaceous, but conquered Kat, "she probably had every right. She's your wife. She was angry. I shouldn't have had those three gin and tonics at breakfast. And she's got a mean left hook too. Please, my baby let it go. And let her go. Did you see her ride off on that beat-up old motorcycle, hanging on to her out-on-the-range-too-long bald headed handy man dude? She was squeezing him like she'd never let got. I wonder how long that has been going on. C'mon, Leah actually looked happy—such poetic contentment. Just let her go. Give her the house, the horses, and the kids. You can stay here, sweetie. It's what we've always wanted. You can invite your big burly man friends over in the evening any time you want to play the Game while I grade papers and paint my toenails. I'm so hungry for you, lover boy. Let's build a life together."

Despite a weak protest from Kat, Luther kissed her fully on her delectable lips and lowered her onto the couch. His desire for this woman was overwhelming.

He would need to explain this situation to the church, his men's group, his attorney, his CPA, his mother, and his three sons, but he knew he had found true love in this red headed lexical powerhouse.

And so, is Luther Free now free? Free from what? Oh yes, he admired his old wife for her beauty and social acceptability. Many would say she was attractive, a trophy, a worthy socialite. But in Dr. Van Dorn, he recognized some raw physical power enhanced by too much gin, perhaps, a great grammatical mind, perfect legs, and some form of liberation from the past which had shaped him, shackled him, shunted, and shellacked him.

Holding Kat in his softly bulging accountant arms, he thought of the pending legal battles, the custody struggle, and the unhappy reaction from his close connections at church. Verily, he saw on Kat's face the battle scars of a long and bitter conflict. Leah might have won the battle, but the war was over.

Free at last, thought Luther Free, free at last.

Kat, nearly crushed under the busy but bulbous bookkeeper's bulk, felt comforted, loved, completely taken.

"Oh, Luther," she grunted into his aromatic right armpit, "I love you so much! Thank you for coming over!"

Then, finally, twisting into fresh air, "Sugar, can you hand me my drink? The full one? Thanks."

Does it matter what you think or I think? The tiny moments of true love articulated by the lucky few—well, let it be.

Adam's Wife Phyllis Comes to Hamilton City

Yes, well, the traditionally manifested fire and flame of passion stuff was probably all true, but Phyllis' burning desire for old Reginald snuffed out like a candle in a hurricane.

Not so long after her last therapy session, Phyllis caught Reggie in a thermonuclear lip-lock with Dr. Kilgear's secretary (of all people) down at the Galloping Grey Goose Saloon and Bistro. That ended her fond affection for Reginald almost immediately.

After beating old Reggie to within an inch of his life, and then after slapping the secretary around a little for good measure, and after being released by the Grand Island police, lovely Phyllis went back to her boudoir, got some of her stuff together, and decided she would go find Adam, her first and truest lover.

What was her motivation? Passion? Anger? Panic? Scorn? Unrequited love? Sense of true romantic purpose? Adam's sexy ways and rugged good lucks? A sense she could salvage the old Black Magic?

Nah. She was out of money. She was flat broke. Phyllis figured she could squeeze a few dollars out of her estranged husband. In her mind, the former professor from Crete College must have a big stash of flashy mashed cash put away, somewhere. Surely.

How did she know where to go? Good question, but Provocative Phyllis had heard through the grapevine, a long one, enhanced by cell phone towers, that Swiss was sinfully and shamefully shacked up with some rich dame, some married b——, in Hamilton City.

She used her last fifty bucks to buy some hamburgers and gas for the twelve hour road trip to North New Mexico—for any future purchases, Phyllis would have to rely on her Master Vice credit card until she found Adam.

The drive was rather uneventful. In some places Highway 34 was icy, and Phyllis encountered an occasional snow shower, a frigid wind, a cough of desperate sleet. The concrete ribbon, bathed in occasional moonlight, was rough, and the stars struggled to shine through the dark and fulsome mists, but she would not be denied.

Phyllis did stop in Dulce, New Mexico, for just a few minutes, to catch the end of a rock show performed by Jamie "The Master" Sego and his band The Rockin' Cessnas. Man those dudes could rock.

Back on the open road! Verily, wolves howled, and owls hooted, unseen banshees shrieked, and the night was frightful. Still, the courageous 1973 Gremlin, with luggage and a bad-looking big, brown, bulgy spare tire strapped on the roof, pierced the darkness, hurrying but smoking mightily through Roswell, like an undaunted, fiery, spooky silver steed.

Near Cimarron, just out of human sight, back in the forest, a family of needy Sasquatches was foraging for beef jerky and half-empty beer bottles. They watched, with obvious interest, an old Gremlin motor car screaming down the frozen road.

"Gruh," said Big Daddy Sasquatch, pointing at the exhaust fumes pouring from Phyllis' car. "Awk!" A tear streamed down Baby Sasquatch's hairy but human-like face. "Gruh," she squeaked. "Gruh. Awk!"

The above passage can be roughly translated thusly: Big Daddy: "Look at that crazy woman driver. Have you found any beer?" Baby: "No. Darn it."

Whatever.

The Big Old Gal drove onward through the night, stopping only occasionally for fuel. She hankered for a Blitz beer, for Reginald's strong arms, for her silky aromatic bathtub.

But the DUI laws were too tough, Reggie had already moved in with his newly-bruised paramour, and Phyllis could never return to her old place and the powerful lusty memories...of what might have been.

Plus, she had received an eviction notice about three days ago for failure to pay rent.

Westward she flew, focused on Adam's big wallet, never giving a moment's reflection to how she could find him or what she would say to him. Her heart was fluttering, but her stomach was growling like a bear's in early March. She stopped in Colorado for more hamburgers, more gas, and then labored through the late lachrymose night. "Oh, Reggie, how could you do this to me?" Finally, she arrived in Hamilton City at the Big Crack of Dawn.

Phyllis pulled into a convenience store after deftly dodging three kids running across the street. Strange, she wondered, did they all have black eyes? She got out of the Gremlin, stretched her massive yet sensual legs, and greeted the clerk. The red head looked tired but approachable. She was stirring a Muchos Mas Grande Gigante' cup of Moonbucks as Phyllis walked up to the counter.

"Hi ya. Name's Phyllis. I'm from Nebraska, lookin' for a guy named Adam Swiss."

"Hi yourself. I'm Charmain. Crazy, but I know Adam. He plays in a rock band with my boyfriend. Man those guys can rock. Swiss lives over in the Hamilton County RV Park with his new girlfriend, Leah."

"Leah, huh? What kind of name is Leah? New girlfriend? I guess you can say I'm the 'old' girlfriend. Hah. Well, he owes me some money. He owes me big time. I gave him the best years of my life. I'm gonna rest up for a while in my car then drive over to see him and make things right. Yeah. Is it okay if I sort of sit in my car out there in your parking lot for an hour or two and get some sleep? I mean, is that okay with the boss or the city or whatever?"

Charmain told her sure, just to park out back by the trash dumpster. The Go Green Recycle truck didn't come till the next day. She also told Phyllis it would be okay to get cleaned up a little in the ladies' restroom.

Phyllis waddled towards the restrooms like a marshmallow snowman.

What a whacko, thought Charmain to herself. Yep. Next to the trashcan is the right place for you, sister. Nice Gremlin you got there, b———.

Meow!

To move the story along, Phyllis freshened up, changed her clothes, pulled out a faded and fuzzy blanket which smelled like 10W-30 motor oil, and slept like a very big baby for about four hours, dreaming of Kilgear, Reggie, and toenail painting and buffing.

She then came back into the store around noon, bought a twelve pack of chilled Blitz Light beer, *"Girl's gotta watch her figure, you know,"* and some pork rinds with her credit card and laboriously returned to her frost-covered and smelly car for lunch.

At about two o'clock, she got directions to the RV Park from Charmain and then decided to walk around the town a bit before heading over to see Adam—who was still her husband.

Phyllis, the Speedo Ghost, and Willie G

Her walk-about-town was pretty uneventful, except she almost got whacked by a bottle of perfume thrown out of a truck by some hell-bent hot-rodder, slipping and sliding around the icy streets, in a beat-up old green Ty-ota.

"Hey you stupid !@#$#% jerk! Watch where you're going!" she screamed, while chasing the truck like a Terminator at full tilt.

That crazy guy got away in a shower of ice chips.

Catching her breath, with a bellyful of beer still sloshing around and disturbing her equilibrium, she dizzily turned and looked directly into a store window at some dummy, actually a mannequin, which seemed to be moving and striking poses. The dummy was dressed up like one of Santa's elves—green fringe and bells and everything—and was modeling handbags for men—or so said the handwritten sign propped up on an easel outside The Espressions Clothing Boutique.

Phyllis had never seen such a thing. The mannequin's movements were hardly noticeable, but yes, he was moving. And strangely, he was half-heartedly smiling at her—faintly, yes, but smiling.

She blinked—and then blinked again. What she saw next changed her life forever. A Chill ran down her spine and the big black wiry hairs on her neck and muscular back stood straight up. Erect. Hard.

Behind Willie—of course she didn't know HIS name yet—was a black curtain, which separated the living mannequin stage and storefront window from the rest of the store. Phyllis couldn't believe what she saw. The atmosphere outside the store darkened. Her breath became icy and misty.

Swaying behind Willie, in front of the black curtain, was, well, it was, uh, er...a waif, a spirit...a GHOST! And not just any ghost. This swaying poltergeist looked oddly familiar. He was old, even in spirit form, and he was wearing a Speedo emblazoned with the Scottish flag. Phyllis was freaked! Now she hadn't learned of the old psychologist's brutal and tragic death yet, but she was quite familiar with the Mystic Lore of the Speedo Clan.

C'mon, ghost or Olympian, who wears a Speedo displaying the Scottish flag while swimming at the YMCA?

Oh, wait, then the Spirit pointed at her, and Phyllis could hear words, though there were no sounds. His grisly, gray, gaping, ghoulish, ghastly lips moved, and she could hear, distinctly, "Have you no shame, woman? Have you no shame?" Mists filled the man-actor staging area, and the shade changed colors several times, but the flag was unflappable. Willie G was nonplussed, even though strange vapors filled in around him.

Ach! All we needed then was Macbeth's witches and a cauldron of bubbling Blitz beer!

Not surprisingly, Phyllis fainted and collapsed in a heap.

Unconscious Phyllis and the Blue Mule
A Prophetic Vision

Phyllis, who was stunned, delirious, or perhaps simply tired, was having a vision.

Perhaps it was in cinemascope. Perhaps it was a diorama. Whatever.

In the vision, or dream, or prophetic trance, she was perched in a Conestoga wagon, facing east. By the looks of the landscape, she was near Chimney Rock, Scottsbluff, Nebraska. Sitting next to her was the young mannequin man.

And...Phyllis was thin and curvy again! Shazam!

Four burros, each wearing a light blue blanket, each with sad-looking eyes, were hitched to the wagon

Phyllis and Willie G were wearing black plants, white shirts, and backpacks. The wagon was standing still; not a bird was chirping, not a coyote yelped, not a moon dog howled.

On one side of them stood a hammerhead roan horse with a handsome rider. Puffing gingerly on a cheroot, he tipped his hat and said, "Howdy, Ma'am. I'm Rowdy B. Yeats. I'll be ridin' east with ya.

I'll be yer ramrod."

Then, an imposing figure, a man carrying a Rogue Phoenix Press published Golden Book, wearing a Blue Beard, and humming "Amazing Grace," rode up on a Big Blue Mule.

"Hi-de-ho! Phyllis, I'm Preacher Hoss. I'll be your trail boss. We're heading east to Omaha to see Brother Steve of the High Life. Old BS knows the Truth. That's a fine mess of burros you got there. You are to marry that young man beside you, and the two of you will spread the word to any who will listen." He hummed a few bars of "Blue Moon," then turned his charging mule to face the rising sun.

Preacher Hoss clucked his tongue, and then the mule, burros, and hammerhead roan started moving eastward. Yes, the High Life awaited them.

The Awakening
Phyllis Finds New Romance!

When Phyllis awoke, she saw a young man staring down at her, a halo about his head. The former dummy was shaking her and trying to give her coffee.

She wasn't sure, but in her dazed state he seemed taller and thinner, surrounded by tentacles, and wearing a black hat.

Suddenly, Phyllis sat bolt upright on the sidewalk, fully alert. She grabbed Willie G by the lapels. "Mister, who are you? I gotta find somebody named Preacher Hoss. Do you know him?"

The mannequin, caught up in a rapturous recognition of the moment and strangely captivated by this crazy fat woman covered by bad tats, exclaimed, "Yes. Yes! I know Preacher Hoss. Come! Come! Let us go to his church. What up?"

Phyllis gave him the good news. "We're getting hitched and then we're gonna be missionaries in Omaha!"

Sounded okay to Willie G. Anything was better than working as a dummy. Besides, maybe he could get a novella or at least an extended short story out of this crazy masque someday.

Preacher Hoss and the Just DOET Wedding

Willie G led Phyllis down Hayden Street, down to the corner at Angus, to Preacher Hoss' church, the Just Daughters of Ethiop Temple.

The Just DOET was a storefront operation, which occupied the space once housing a feed store on the Hamilton City town square. Willie G pulled the hanging brass bells tied to the plate glass door, which looked much like the entryway to any convenience mart. Preacher Hoss, who Phyllis recognized immediately even though his beard was not blue, opened the door.

"How may I help you, my children?" gently queried the bearded, be-robed cleric, who smelled faintly of patchouli incense and carefully carried a golden book in his right hand.

Phyllis spoke excitedly: "Preacher, uh, ah, er, ah, er, I was watching this here dummy move around inside that there clothing store across the street. Then I saw a ghost, and then I passed out, then you were in the dream, then I saw burros and this young fellow here, then you told us to get married, to go to Omaha, and convert sinners!"

Preacher Hoss grew pale and quivered, but then he gave a great shout.

"Hallelujah! Sweet Mother of Just Ethiop! My prophecies have come to pass."

"Come in, my children. I will marry you, lay hands upon your noggins to exorcise the ghostly demon, and tell you about the mission of our church. Please come in, come in."

So Preacher Hoss drew the blinds, locked the door, and, with great care, set down the book he had been studying (*The Philip Dolly Affair*).

His church, which contained exactly twenty-three folding chair seats, was empty. But there were hundreds of old boxes scattered around containing clothes, shoes, Big Foot memorabilia, light fixtures, knick-knacks, candles, and eighties-era electronics.

"Excuse the mess, my children," said Preacher Hoss. "We are having a rummage sale later this week to raise money for our foundation."

Preacher Hoss explained his ministry worked with women who suffered from crazy husbands and doctors and counselors.

He saw himself as a kind of wise Solomon who knew his church must heed a Grand Calling, a Holy Purpose. He wanted to establish a new church in Omaha and bring peace and sanctity to the women folk, the sisters and daughters, who suffered there.

"You two have been touched by the Spirit of Ethiop—that is what brought you to me. Go to Omaha in a covered wagon drawn by four burros. Find Brother Steve, who ministers in the Church of the High Life. He will give you succor as you work among the unholy drunken messes."

Well, Phyllis and Willie G bought into their new mission, their new life plan, without much resistance. The fiery speech of Preacher

Hoss could not be ignored or resisted or denied. Still reeling from her confrontation with Kilgear's ghost and the nasty noxious knock on her noggin, Phyllis had great empathy for women who had suffered from the toxic contamination of men, and Willie—uh, you know about Willie already.

And in her new religious fervor, Phyllis had forgotten completely about 1) her need for cash and beer and; 2) her estranged husband, handy man Adam Swiss.

[Just a note: Adam forgot about Phyllis about two minutes after gazing at Leah Free for the first time. Very easily.]

So the three zealots prayed together, shouted, waved hands and elbows in the air, cried, and finally collapsed, exhausted, in a writhing pile. Preacher Hoss, pulling himself together and speaking in an African tongue, laid his soft feely hands everywhere on Phyllis, and she squealed a porcine squeal as her thousand demons fled.

Willie G. noticed goodly Preacher Hoss certainly enjoyed laying hands on

Phyllis, but the stoic-yet-pliable mannequin man said nothing.

Then, ceremoniously, the pastor held hands with the new couple, looked quickly down the street towards Moonbucks, and pronounced them man and wife, "In the name of Holy Ethiopia," and bade them good luck on their mission to Omaha.

Moments later, the newlyweds were shopping for new clothes, backpacks, Grand Canyon-style burros, and a covered wagon.

Not long after, Preacher Hoss stroked his beard, lit an unfiltered smoke, picked up his *Phil Dolly* novel, and walked down to Moonbucks for an iced coffee, joyous at the new conversions. Now he had twenty-three parishioners and two missionaries in the church.

Time for a love offering, thought the preacher. Some Big Love.

His blue jackass, tied to a No Parking sign, smiled as the Preacher walked by. Yippee-yi-yo-ki-yay!

A Parrot, dressed like a small Caribbean pirate, sat on the blue jackass' saddle, eyeing Preacher Hoss with some suspicion. Not much more to say.

Leah in the RV Park

So, was Leah feeling lethargic, beaten, forsaken, cast into the pit like one of John Milton's fallen angels in *Paradise Lost*? Not at all. A few days had passed since the Rumble in the Restaurant. Most of the discoloring on her knuckles had dissipated. Late on a Thursday morning, she was applying polish to her ten perfect toenails, waiting for Adam Swiss to return from repairing a broken screen down at the Rec Hall. She had a severe, powerful attachment to that rough-looking, aging maintenance man, that's for sure. She couldn't help but think of him, her sculpted lover, who was pounding away with a big, firm hammer, or caulking furiously, while she rubbed sweet, aromatic coconut-flavored lotion into her freshly-shaven calves.

Her new pasta and cheese soup existence had been good so far. She had spent the past thirteen days straightening up the pots and pans in Adam's travel trailer, running down to the Doorgreens to stock up on toiletries (the closet-sized bathroom was quaint but crowded), reading panicky text message from friends on her smart phone, and looking forward to each moment with her musical, magical, working-man love machine.

She had learned the names of her neighbors—most of whom could be seen keeping an eye on Adam's aluminum love shack around the clock.

Could it be focused love—fresh, powerful, aromatic, sensual, pure, and basic—was more powerful than economic propensity? Didn't Leah miss her old domestic life at all? What about her sons?

—Intermission—

McDougal, Owner and Operator,
McDougal's Big Red Burgers

They mock me...

Ach, I live life the way I want.

Spending my days above a hardware store in Hamilton City

In a small apartment with steam heat.

Ach, I doan give a dom about movies, politics, romance, or fashions.

I mind me own business, ya see, I sell a few burgers and have no debts

Yah, and you'll never see me with an iPod or a smurph phone, you know.

Cause, quite simply put, I doan want to speak with anyone after work—it's all been said...

What unholy Text, what demented script, what sick screenplay must ye all be readin'? Chinchillas rule the world now, running round and round in their self-forged wheels without hope.

Oh, sure, once I marched with the red berets—once I believed in politics—once I thought I could change the world—where did it get me?

As long as the people can get a burger and fries, even at me high prices, well they'll be happy—mutton heads they be in a beef-eatin' world!

Oh, sure I'll sit on a park bench readin' a book about Marx or Shaw or Kochenderfer or Thompson or Steincamp or Brown or Moulton or Wesley or Moore or David Jones or Hoyt or Hall or Paddison or Jensen or Wells or the Lord himself.

And I'll enjoy a conversation about emics and etics while I'm French-fryin' an onion or two, or watching me burgers splatter and spit. Ah!

You want a veggie burger? Ha, you silly !@#$%. Sushi? Go down the street, get out of me sight. A latte'? Oh, laddie, the world is doomed. Ye cannot even sustain your own conversations without checking your smurphone!

So you believe in love. Ach, it is a capitalist fantasy, boy, meant to cost money and drain your emotions into a puddle of poverty. Ach!

And they'll mock me 'cause I can't talk about sports or popped culture.

As for music—how many times do yah need to hear Aerosmith or Korn or Justa Beaver? It's all the same, laddie, they are exploitin' ya and ya doan even know it.

Ach, they mock me

And my life, well, it is fine.

Ach.

I won't be flimflammed, flummoxed, fanaticized, flamboyant or fooled.

Love in the RV Park

Sure I weep frequently—me loneliness is a freezing fever—there is no woman of grace and loving beauty, no queen of my humid dreams, to wipe the sad, surging tears from me old rheumy eyes now or before.

I have not a memory of tenderness, or a birthday cake, or a walk in the park through golden April sunlight.

But I've had a few good beers here and there, that be for sure.

Me heart broke like a shattered light bulb a long, long time ago…

I'll never follow the script of your play. So you think this is the new age, the apocalypse, a harmonious society? Human nature is ancient, lad, and always predictable. Nothing is different. There's just drinking, loving, and eating. In that order! Oh, lad, I'll ride me motorbike alone in the crisp and coughing desert, through the curved copper canyons, pulsing upon the steamed and shimmering highway, and create my own sad, still poetry till I can do it no more. Go watch your movies and relish text messages from your chinchilla friends. What are the outcomes ye seek? Better fountains of grief than servitude, laddie.

Oh. Ya best stop by for a good Red Burger Special. You'll feel better and live longer.

Current Status of Old Free Domicile and the Boys...

Perhaps this might be a good time to get caught up on what had transpired with the extant Free domestic unit. And much had happened quickly. An attorney from the Missouri River Boat law firm of Ravitch, Biden, Fish, Clinton and Geitner called Leah soon after the Luncheon Bludgeon, and advised her of Luther's terms. Very simply, not much would happen for a while. For the time being, Luther wanted a "legal" separation. He would deposit eight thousand dollars monthly into her checking account. She could have open access to the house and the boys and her car—and he would continue paying all her bills and infrastructure and health insurance costs. At the end of one year, if they were not reconciled, they would split up the assets and go their separate ways. Well, Leah agreed to most of this. But she made sure her mother was given permission to move into the house and more or less manage the boys' daily lives and be paid a one thousand dollar weekly stipend for her efforts.

How were the boys holding up? They hadn't missed a beat. Mike, Robbie, and Chip welcomed this obvious freedom from constant parental influence; they got along well with their grandma; Leah would be around plenty of the time to give them extra cash; and they were pretty much away at school, sleep-overs, or sporting events 24/7 anyway. As long as they had iPads, iPhones, Gameboys, cable TV, Nitflix, and all other portals to meaningless but soothing virtual reality, they would be "on board" with the separation.

No one would be "thrown under the bus." Absolutely not.

Plus, as the oldest boy pointed out to the youngest during a private sibling caucus, if their parents split up and re-married other people, things might actually get better. Then, each of them would receive twice as many Christmas and birthday presents in the future since there would be so many new relatives.

Such was American life, my friends...

Val Hamilton
Just a Nice Lonely Guy

Val lived in a nice Class C motorhome. He resided only a few spaces down from Adam Swiss and the gal Val had come to view as the "World's Hottest Chick."

Val's Wife, a former weight lifting champion, left him for another woman a few years ago. Val was philosophical about this event even to this day. His wife had never actually settled into the domestic life. She was always at a happy hour, or hockey games, or playing softball with other out-of-shape individuals who wore their softball championship t-shirts to work and church.

Once Val caught Wife using his razor. She was trimming her moustache. Val told her she should have left the moustache alone. Probably wasn't a good idea to suggest this to her, Val.

One day Wife announced to Val that she had found true though forbidden love with a bowling alley snack bar receptionist named Margaret—a white female, forty-five, who still lived at home.

Margaret was an exciting person who kept herself occupied at work by "Liking" on Facebook, playing videogames, and downloading music for her mp3 player.

Anyway, Wife and Margaret, a handsome couple better suited to smart phone reality than the daily grind of adult responsibility, realized great happiness and decided to move in together. Note—they didn't reside in the RV Park.

Val sold the house, gave his wife half the cash, and bought his motorhome.

Val had never been happier. He ran each day and stayed in terrific condition for a sixty-three year old man.

He made his living writing small articles for online comedy magazines and newspapers, and his self-published bowling alley romance novel was currently selling six copies a month on Amazon.

His small refrigerator could manage a twelve pack of beer without strain. He enjoyed a hearty can of chicken soup at the end of the day, or a tuna fish sandwich, and slept quite peacefully now on his fold-down bed.

But something had happened to Val recently, something BIG, something which had disrupted his calm and uneventful life.

Here is how it all went down.

A few weeks ago, he helped a friend move. The friend asked Val if he wanted some book cases which were about to be relegated to the scrap heap or local Goodwill store, just tired yet-still-productive victims of the move.

Val, a tightwad and never able to pass up a deal, took home the bookcases, even though he had scant space for such furniture. With a little time on his hands, (Val had just finished carefully editing his latest eBook and print-on-demand novel), he decided to prime and repaint the shelves so they would match the rich décor in his motor home.

Everything went okay on Val's first visit to the paint store. He bought a gallon of primer from a championship t-shirt wearing big-boned woman with tribal tats whom he recognized as one of his wife's former softball teammates.

Sure, things went okay priming the bookcases. He took his time, gave them a couple of coats, and actually made them quite presentable.

But a week later—well, that's when the trouble started.

Val returned to the paint store to pick up a gallon of "molasses," a dark brown colored latex enamel mix. A new paint technician was waiting for him.

The Pretty Paint Girl was different. She was thin, was wearing a smock, and had closely-cropped blond hair.

She had a dainty ruby nose piercing and bright orange lips.

Val, for the love of heaven, don't look at those perfect lips! Too late! Too late! Too late!

When Val first entered the store, she was occupied doing some work at the cash register. When she turned to see what Val wanted, she saw her face in Val's eyes. And she stopped breathing. Her hands dropped to her sides, her paint can "key" opener rattled to the floor. And Val could not speak when he saw her looking at him. Her nametag read simply, Marcia.

Their catatonic trance-like dialogue follows as it occurred:

Marcia: May I help you?

Val: Yes, I uh need some paint mixed. Would you be able to help me?

Marcia: What? *Ringing in her pretty ears—just small diamond posts through the lobes.*

Val: Yes, I, uh, need some paint mixed. Would you be able to help me? *Wishing he was dressed better.*

Marcia: May I help you? *Zoned out!*

Val: Yes, I, uh, ah need some paint mixed. Would you be able to help me? *I wish you would kiss me!*

Marcia: What? *Seeing only a glory shining about Val.*

Val: Yes, I, uh, ah, uh, need some paint mixed. Would you be able to help me?

Marcia: What? Ya, of course. What kind do you want? *I wish you would kiss me!*

Val: Doh, "molasses" in enamel. *Losing interest in the paint—seeing only the outline of her firm legs enclosed in tight blue jeans.*

Marcia: Ya, sure, I can make it up for you.

Val stuttering: Are you from South Africa? Your voice—your accent—you—you are—all beautiful. *Weird—Val had never heard a South African speak before.*

Marcia: Ya. I have been in America eighteen years. Ya. I am a citizen now. *She worked on paint mixture for Val and started up the mixing machine. I wish you would kiss me right now!*

Paint mixing machine throbbed, vibrated, hummed, and then grunted softly and quit, exhaling and smiling.

Marcia, panting slightly, opened up the can to check color.

Marcia: Oh, darn it. I've mixed up the wrong paint. I'm so sorry. I'll have to redo it. *I wish you would kiss me!*

Anyway, Marcia redid the paint mix. Val, in a nervous frenzy, shook her hand, paid for the paint, and went home. Val could not sleep. In the next three weeks, he bought forty-six unnecessary gallons of paint from the Paint Store.

Things got worse. When he painted the bookshelves, his mind

slipped slightly. He believed he was painting great art, her portrait, the Alps, a visual hymn to Marcia. He became fixated on the bookshelves and loved them like their children.

Marcia continued to make mixing errors at the paint store. She was transfixed by that image of Val standing at the counter, her face reflected in his eyes.

Ya, she mused to herself. I must read *Jane Eyre* again!

He and Marcia could be the world's great love story. He was tall, lean, and had a stubbly Euro-chin other men only dreamed of. She was the South African Paint Girl—a pixie in white, stunningly beautiful and normally quite confident, serene, and poised.

But neither could speak—they could only gaze at each other and utter pleasantries each time Val stopped at the paint store to buy more paint. Marcia never wondered what Val was doing with all the paint.

Why didn't somebody say something?

Sometimes, during the weeks which followed, mid-afternoon, Val heard noises outside his Class C motorhome—crunching leaves, closing car doors, dogs barking—and in his infatuated condition, he believed Marcia had found out where he lived and was going to knock on his door... .

At night, when Val lay on his bed in the Class C and looked up through the nice transparent skylight, he saw Marcia in the heavens, in-constellated, and he wished he could hold her in his arms.

Each day, Marcia hoped Val would come by and order some more paint. He usually did.

Why didn't somebody say anything? Something? Anything!

Bob Zontarg
Band on the Run

After a few emails, phone calls, Moonbucks coffees, and grocery store check-out line conversations, Adam Swiss and Dan, the Ice Cream Man, who had met each other after a Swiss gig at Moonbucks, decided it was time to form a serious band. They knew of two other musicians who might be interested in the project—Jann Contento, a jazz drummer and dean of institutional research at the community college, and Bob Zontarg, lead guitarist and lead custodian, also from Copperfield Community.

On a snowy mid-December afternoon, when most right-thinking people were out Christmas shopping or returning Hanukkah gifts, the foursome got together to talk about their musical careers. They met over at Zontarg's doublewide, just across from the RV Park on Edison Avenue.

Zontarg had played with the Little Colorado River Band for quite a few years. The LCRB had three or four gigs down at the Copper Coin Saloon and even opened up once for the Alabama Satellites at the North New Mexico State Fair back in the late eighties. Zontarg was not a disciplined guitarist, but he knew barre chords and chromatic and pentatonic scales. And, he knew how to work distortion pedals and big amps.

Dan was a very primitive bass player who liked to quarter note his way through every song. He felt the best music ever made came from the Ramones. Dan had a collection of eighty-nine dollar bass guitars he had purchased from Bass Player's Friend Discount Music House. Most were of Asian descent.

Jann was clearly the most experienced musician of the group. Years ago, he had played in an alternative band with Val Hamilton and probably lost half of his hearing playing on Mill Avenue over in Arizona with Patty Cook and the Slip.

Then, more recently, he had drummed for a rockabilly band called Jann and the Moondoggs for several decades. The big break never came, though, and Jann finally got tired of playing free gigs at Moonbucks.

He was quite wary of this new project.

Jann was recently engaged to be married. Jann had bought a new house and was looking for a better job or promotion. He didn't really have the time to practice. But Swiss had convinced him to come to the meeting.

So, after straightening up his collection of Beatles memorabilia and kissing his fiancé on the cheek, he hopped in his truck and headed over to Zontarg's. After finding Zontarg's joint from a map sketched out by Swiss, Contento grimaced and inwardly groaned. This !@#$% guy lives in the ghetto, thought Contento to himself.

Swiss, of course, was a fair rhythm player and had a suitable voice with a limited range. His idea for the band? Half originals, half covers.

Sitting around a table, each with a bottle of beer, they began planning. They were a relaxed group, hungry to find musical success after years of rock and roll frustration.

Swiss: Well, Jann, what is your vision for the band?

Jann: I'd like to find some paying gigs, maybe some weddings or retirement parties. I'd like to dress nice, like the Beatles did, with white shirts and ties. No freebies. Or not many. A ratio of at least four paying gigs for each fundraiser. And please, no Moonbucks or birthday parties. I hope we can play some Beatles covers. Or Jazz.

Dan: Nah, that's too old school. We need to play more modern stuff. Did I show you my new tat of a Gibson Flying V? I'm getting a five string bass in case we play any cyberpunk!

Zontarg picked at a guitar while his Marshall Stack screeched in the background. He was working on some full step hammer on.

Swiss: Bob, can you turn that thing down?

Zontarg turned knob from seven to five.

Zontarg: Charmain, baby, can you bring me another beer?

Charmain: Do you guys know any Frampton?

Dan jumped up and belted out "Feel like We Do" bass line.

Charmain jumped up, danced on table, fell off, got back up, and started singing.

Bob wailed away on his guitar.

Charmain: How about Nazareth? "Love Hurts," man, love hurts bad. Real bad. Dude.

The phone rang. No one answered. A voice message, from neighbor Eastermann, complained about loud shrieking !@#$% music.

A car pulled up with a Queen CD blaring from the rattling stereo. Then a tinny door slammed. Buzz Clocker, Zontarg's girlfriend from the old days, way old days, and current bartender at the Copper Coin, lunged at Zontarg's front door with a case of Blitz beer bottles under her arm. Buzz stumbled, got up, stumbled, and then crawled up the steps through the door.

She hadn't been drinking yet this afternoon. At least not much.

Yes, the Queen music continued blaring from her car stereo.

Buzz: Hey! I heard you guys were gonna be jamming. I thought we'd make it a party! Do you know "Cat Scratch Fever"?

Zontarg jumped up, turned the amp knob to eleven, and belted out some opening riffs.

Buzz and Charmain were singing, off key: The first time that I caught it I was just ten years old...

Buzz went outside to fetch a beer. She left the case out in a snow bank to keep the bottles good and cold.

Some random chick with a beat-up old Afro hairdo who wandered in from the street, shouted: Hey do you guys know any Grand Funk? Man I love "Foot stomping Music," man. Man, Grand Funk could Rock, man. Hey, dudes, I was, like, married to Mark Farner once, man. Really. Like. Awesome. Absolutely.

Dan: Zontarg—you are playing it in the wrong key!

Zontarg finished his second bottle of Blitz: !@#$%. No I'm not. I saw some !@#$% guy playing it on YouTube. Aw !@#$%. The battery went completely dead in my fuzz box!

The phone rang wearily yet again. No one answered. A voice message from another distant neighbor, Davies, complained about loud music.

Buzz and Charmain lit up smokes. They had been drinking soundly, laughing and singing arm in arm. Dan leered at Buzz as she swayed provocatively in the smoky half-light. Her shiny fresh asphalt black lipstick made her so, so, kissable.

Contento and Swiss exited. Contento drove away in old Toyota truck. Swiss rode off into swirling snowflakes on the DT-1, heading home urgently to loving Leah.

Dan: I told you that !@#$% song is in A!

Charmain: Hey, do you guys remember Head East? *Flat as a Pancake?* Those guys could Rock! Have you seen the Kings and Queens cover "Never Been Any Reason" on YouTube? Dude. Those chicks can Rock! Head East man, Head East. Dude.

Dan: !@#$%. Dude!

Zontarg: !@#$%. I thought it was in F. Do you know any Zep? "Whole Lotta Love"? He pounded out more opening riffs, knob turned to fifteen. Bob finished drinking his seventh bottle of Blitz and was in great form.

The phone rang. No one answered. The voice message was from Becky, who was looking for Jann.

This incident prompted Jann to get his own cell phone.

Fifteen minutes later, Dan and Buzz were making out on the couch. As they rolled around, pawing each other mercilessly, smooching and grunting like wolverines, the new couple smashed bags of pretzels and dollar store chips, knocked over half empty Blitz bottles, and nearly set the place on fire when they kicked over an ashtray.

Fortunately, the smoldering newspaper in the trashcan thankfully self-extinguished before a blaze began. Yass, just like Dan and Buzz's smoldering passion, the potential conflagration simply gave it up. Pffft!

Soon, Dan was snoring with robust, sustainable, and strategic vigor. Buzz, slobbering and happy, wasn't far behind.

Screeching feedback came out of Zontarg's Marshall Stack—he had leaned his pock-marked and cigarette-burned old Ibanez guitar against the amp so that he and Charmain could go outside for a smoke.

Then two nicely dressed missionaries pulled up on their bicycles. Braving the pending snow storm, they had come to visit with Brother Zontarg about his waning beliefs.

The screaming feedback, distorted music, and shrieks of sinful laughter and good times compelled them to rethink their mission and re-mount their two-wheeled steeds. The missionaries exited left—quickly, very quickly.

Brother Ethan to Brother Spenser: What do we tell the Bishop about that crazy place? Man, those guys can Rock!

Dan, finally, who took an urgent break from the omnipresent Big Buzz and sleepy time to lope down the hall towards the bathroom, flipped the amp head switch to "Off." The speakers stopped screaming and the amp head quit smoking.

Dan picked up his ninth bottle of Blitz and sat on the now-awake Buzz's lap, cooing in the big woman's left ear while she tilted her head back and laughed her crazy laugh.

Bob and Charmain, a happy couple, sat outside on the snow-covered doublewide's front steps and enjoyed non-filtered cigarettes, making crab nebulae smoke clouds in the paling sky.

Zontarg: Man, I love to rock.

Charmain: I love you, Bob. Man, you can rock. Um. Smiling, she played air guitar joyously.

The happy rockers continued smooching and nuzzling. Snowflakes swirled around them as the sun, a faint and bleary pink disk, sank and brought peace to the neighborhood.

A nearly-empty case of Blitz beer reposed in a shadowy snow bank.

Rock music and beer. What else is there, man? Dude. Long Live Rock!

Leah and Adam See the Lights

The total mid December snowfall in Hamilton City was about four and a half inches—a little below average but enough for most.

Activity quieted down in the RV Park. The few days surrounding Christmas were pretty uneventful. The holiday season brought out decorations, carolers, and hard drinking, and a few weak and poorly disguised efforts at spirituality.

In the spirit of cultural diversity, multiculturalism, increased transparency, and accountability, it should be mentioned some RV Park residents celebrated Kwanzaa, Hanukkah, Yule, Brazen Mutant Squirrel Sacrifices, and other festivities associated with the winter solstice during this time frame.

One slushy evening, Adam and Leah rode the DT-1 motorcycle around the park, then up and down, up and down, a few streets in town to look at the holiday lights.

Passing by her old mansion, she noticed her mother, or at least she guessed it had been her mother, had put up a tree with lights inside the front bay window, and a new Doorgreens quality wreath hung on the front entryway. Strangely, when they rattled by the old place, Leah didn't feel a twinge of guilt, or sadness, or Christmas nostalgia. She could think of nothing she wanted out of the old barn—except maybe her expensive espresso maker and a few bottles of even pricier wine.

As they moved down the street, carefully dodging patches of ice, she playfully bit the exposed bit of sagging skin on Adam's neck. They were both wearing half helmets. This newly developed signal caused him to purposefully turn left at the next intersection, head back to the RV Park, and, after passing two cold-looking missionaries on bicycles, idle up to their own trailer. After carrying Leah across the threshold to the aluminum Bower of Bliss, they tumbled into a nest of tangled sheets and pillows and blankets and... Well, my friends, they had a holiday.

Eastermann Takes a Present to Charmain

After a few more December beer and grocery runs down to the convenience store, and believing the bouncy Charmain was furtively flirting with him, Eastermann decided he would take her a Christmas present. Seemed the right thing to do.

For some reason, Frank got into his mind the surging idea that Charmain was interested in him and that she was expecting something from him. Perhaps losing his grip on long-term hopeless bachelor reality, Frank believed she was going to give him a carton of cigarettes for Christmas—nicely packaged in red aluminum foil with a shiny green bow.

He had this strange fantasy she spent half of her workday, at the store, looking out the window, hoping he would drive up.

Now Frank was a decent looking guy for his age, but he was no spring chicken. Charmain was a little heavy, but still had her curves and looked pretty !@#$% good in tight, sequined jeans. What would they look like together in one of those annual Christmas family photographs that get mailed out?

He had a special mental image of himself licking postage stamps to stick on the envelopes—lovely gold foil envelopes containing high quality Frank and Charmain Season's Greetings cards for their friends and family.

Even so, for a couple of weeks running, there had been this philosophical struggle taking place in Frank's head.

The following opposing elements of this struggle can be summarized briefly below.

1. There is no fool like an old fool.
2. Or—Dude, when love comes around, you've got to go for it!

Frank had no idea about a proper present for Charmain, but he had learned from television commercials that women always liked expensive perfume. He took twenty dollars down to the corner Doorgreens. There were sixty-seven such stores in Hamilton City. He boldly walked through the door into the seasonal candle and potpourri aromas and asked the clerk—wow, what a knock out she was in her scanty, frilly blouse—about perfume.

Well, the lady told Frank, DK was favored by most sophisticated women this year, especially the eleven ounce size, and his girlfriend would surely appreciate a large DK.

"Ah, yes," said Frank, with an unmatchable cosmopolitan flair. "I'll take a bottle of big DK. Please give me the biggest DK you've got."

Frank also sensed he impressed this gal. He noticed she looked much like Charmain. He saw she was wearing a black oak leaf brassiere beneath her white blouse. He considered why she dressed this way. He wondered if the clerk was interested in him. She was very pleasant and helpful. Um.

After gift-wrapping the small but potent box—a nice touch, thought Frank, while signing the tag "Love, Frank"—she methodically and rhythmically rang him up at the cash register.

"That'll be $77.91, including tax." She smiled sweetly, emitting strange and fetching aromas, her sumptuous and anticipatory bosom pulsing with vigor beneath the frilly blouse.

Frank flinched and nearly fainted, but it was too late now. He got out a credit card, paid his debt to society, and left in his Toyota truck a few minutes later.

Man, DK is expensive! he thought to himself. He was stunned by the price but happy to be on this romantic mission. Frank was sure she would like the big DK he would give her.

So, as he drove along through the slush, he thought about how he would give her the DK—what she would say—what his next move might be—what she might be wearing—her friendly smile—those cute jelly shoes—the dimples when she smiled—wondered if Chairman cuddled up with a book and a cat at home—apple cinnamon candles burning in each room—under a blanket, drinking hot tea on winter evenings—watching old black and white movies—her sighs and day dreams—would she hug him—phone numbers—calls late at night, just checking in— email addresses—did she have a family in town—what this all might mean—a random jumble of excited, happy, warm and loving thoughts filled him with glad profusion. He grasped his potent DK with gusto.

He turned the corner, headed towards the convenience store gas pumps, smiling, eager...and saw her standing outside in the snow, wearing furry boots and tight jeans...and [Ahg!] making out with a guy in a lip-stick smudged and holey wife-beater shirt.

95

Charmain's right hand was around the dude's neck, flexing and holding him tightly.

At that moment, they were giving each other a wet tongue-licking, their breathing steamy and fervent in the damp winter air, a foggy mist enveloping both of their panting, eager, and squirming faces.

Her left hand dangled a burning cigarette. Menacing ashes were rancorously falling on the icy patch surrounding them. Charmain and her firm, ardent Lover were silhouetted like a lustful, hungry couple atop a sagging, decadent wedding cake.

Frank also noticed the loser had a Gibson guitar tattooed on his forearm.

Frank was sick! Horrified, he gunned the truck, spraying ice and water all over Charmain and Dan, spinning and roaring out of the parking lot. As he slid out of this Den of Perdition, he nearly ran over two young men on bicycles.

They shouted at him but did not curse.

A block or two away by now, Frank looked down at his shriveled bottle of DK. He grabbed it and tossed it through the open window. He had to get to the Copper Coin Saloon bad. Real Bad. And fast.

Charmain and Dan watched the taillights disappear down the street. She thought she saw some small object fly out the window. It was immediately run over and smashed into smithereens by a USB truck.

"Who's that crazy dude?" asked Dan. "He got me all !@#$% wet!"

Charmain, wiping off a big splotch of melting white snow from her forehead and mouth, replied with a storekeeper's wisdom, "Ah, the old nut comes in here about every other day and buys a twelve pack of Blitz. He never makes eye contact. What a mess. Maybe he's drunk or something. !@#$%! Have you got band practice tonight, sweet thing? Be sure to say hi to Bob for me."

Frank, you should have listened to number one.

He had never liked wedding cake, anyway.

Leah's Quiet Evening in the Trailer While Adam Fixed a Washing Machine:
A Poetic Fragment

Though snow fell most Decembers, this storm had a rusty smell
Adobe slowly faded into murky spirit mists
Leah spent such evenings weaving garlands of lowland winter blooms

With gracious hands so soft and warm they seemed heated by the summer sun, farther south but still simmering
Their room was filled with lace, lamps, and yesterday
Cotton gauze flowed smoothly down her form

Her pursed red lips whispered to someone—but Adam could not hear her soft yet painful cries.

A keenness in her look presumed the chilly night's attention, and made the coals burn mildly

She waited for a waking dream—and then brightened, finding a working bee lodged deep within her flowers

Arching her feet beneath the padded quilt, she waited, hungry, for her always-loving man

Jeffrey Ross

And Leah's heart beat the steady rhythm of love, sweet love, potent love, total love, hungry love, forceful love, and womanly love

And later, he will come to her, a powerful, musky animal presence, moaning heavily in the moist but sleepy night, making her complete…

A webbed aesthetic unity greater than this or any cosmos…

Sol on Christmas Morning

Old Sol rolled out of bed on Christmas morning. He had been up late, again, kept awake by that same noisy rock band, which must have been partying hearty on Christmas Eve. But beautiful, bountiful Blitz beer had eased him into slumber.

He looked at the clock through foggy eyes and found to his delight it was only 7:33 am.

After padding over to the kitchen and buttering up a raw bagel for the microwave, Sol opened up the refrigerator and reached out to grasp a beer. Hesitating, he considered the special nature of this day and, out of respect, decided to wait till eight am for his first Blitz.

Sol peeked through the bamboo blinds to see what was going on over at the exotic Swiss ranch. He noticed the motorcycle was parked out front, covered in snow (why didn't !@#$% Swiss cover that thing?) and steam rising from the furnace vent, but no other movement or activity was indicated.

He wondered about the loving taking place over there but couldn't work up much of an imaginative fantasy. Sol was basically a decent man.

Sol sat down in his favorite chair and worked on the bagel, chewing gingerly with his sensitive teeth. He probably needed a root canal or two but wouldn't spend the money.

"Well, h——," said Sol. "A new year is coming. Maybe things will look up. I feel good."

Sol decided he should approach the coming New Year with an open and curious mind. He could expand his horizons and think differently, more positively.

Perhaps he would watch BBC or the black and white movie channel once in a while.

Importantly, last night, while studying *A Wonderful Life* on the TV, Sol had this inspirational notion to start working on a book about women.

He was now keeping a yellow legal pad of notes on the coffee table for recording his valuable insights and observations. Sol usually had the best insights after a few beers, so he would have to wait till nine or ten am to start work on the book today, Christmas.

Still waiting for eight am to arrive, and growing thirsty, Sol glanced around his six by four foot living room area. He hadn't decorated much for the holidays this year. Ah, just too much trouble to get all my Christmas stuff out, grumped old Sol to himself.

But he had nicely displayed the five Christmas cards he received from his distant relatives—and the one from Swiss and his hot girlfriend. Strangely enough, Sol had also received a card, actually card number seven, from his son—the one who was doing hard time in the Clovis State Prison. And, against his better judgment, Sol had placed a small wreath in the window looking out towards Edison Ave.

Ding Ding! Eight o'clock arrived after another agonizingly apathetic fifteen minutes passed. Happily—and thirsty for Good Cheer—Sol reestablished his age-old acquaintance with Blitz.

After refreshing himself with four or five of his newly-refrigerated, malty friends, Sol obtained a moment of credible crystal clairvoyant clarity and began listing several of his keen observations, albeit in a deformed, desultorily manner, certainly lacking a meaningful methodology, about women folk:

1. Women get mad if you look at 'em, and get madder if you don't look at 'em.

2. What women truthfully want in a husband is a big, fat, thick wallet.

3. A man marries a woman hoping she will stay the same—a woman marries a man knowing she can change him.

4. A married woman may fake happiness, but she is always looking for someone better. (Part of the Marital-Shopping Domesticity Complex described by Roz [2011] and other social science scholars!)

5. Women have no imagination.

6. Women go shopping hoping to find something cute. Men go shop for the one thing they need at one store and then go home. !@#$%.

7. The first thing a woman says after her divorce? "Well, I better lose about sixty pounds before I start dating again."

8. What a woman most wants out of life is a massive cookie cutter suburban home and a framed family photo on her desk at work.

9. Lovin' or shoppin'? Ha!

10. Women would rather have gift cards than DK.

"Ha!" said callously creative craftsman Mr. Davies out loud. "Well, probably no one will want to read this stuff, but these are the whispered truths which could solve half of the world's problems"!

For about five minutes, Sol felt pretty good. Then he saw a few kids on new bicycles riding down Edison Avenue, and he started thinking. A few moments later, he saw a happy young couple walking their Irish Springer dogs with Christmas ornament collars, and he stopped drinking. Turning around, and seeing the greeting card from his son in prison, Old Sol was sinking.

Needing air bad, he pushed through the door and sat on a snow-covered lawn chair. Rocking his gnarly old head in his crusty and wrinkled hands, Sol wept like a baby, sobbing, heaving, and groaning. Nearly panic-stricken, Sol watched his hot tears plinking on the icy patio.

He thought of his wife, his children, his miserably smug life.

For a few moments, anyway.

Snow began falling more steadily. A breeze died. Bells from the nearby St. Arnold's Catholic Church reverberated in the damp and foggy morning stillness.

Regaining his composure, feeling no catharsis, no redemption— only the chilly morning air—Sol went back inside and opened another Blitz buddy.

Desperately seeking fusion.

Funny, he thought to himself, *when I was younger, I said many a time that beer was my only friend. Ach. I was a prophet.*

Sol flipped on his big screen TV and rambled through the channels quickly and methodically. He found himself talking back to a newscast on CNN. "Those people are !@#$%," thought Sol out loud. "!@#$%. All they got is shiny teeth, talking heads and beautiful legs.

One more dog rescue story and I'm gonna scream!"

Sol changed his mind about the focus of his emerging life's work. He gave up on the woman analysis project. Something in his brief but thorough examination of the female psyche, the girlish purpose, the womanly wanton distraction, had triggered bad memories—made him soft and nostalgic.

Now Sol was filled with inspiration from fabulous, frothy, foamy, fabulous Blitz.

He must write, respond to the muse, and listen to the conductor in his head.

He saw his forthcoming novel as a block of granite with a statue inside just waiting to be chiseled out, chiseled free.

I wonder what Swiss was doing, Sol asked himself. Man, Leah Free is a looker!

Suddenly, with newly-awakened and robust vigor, he decided he would comment on various aspects of American culture which were presented to him on TV.

Yes, this might be a best seller. Before opening yet another refreshing and invigorating Blitz, he sketched out a new list, on the legal pad, about things which were powerfully affecting him. He decided to ask himself questions he could answer later when he was more fully empowered. Grabbing a pencil and the yellow pad, his ideas, his queries, flowed like magic:

1. Why do these guys get paid to wear shirts and ties and talk about sports and dogs all day? Kid's games and they make all that d—— money!

2. Why does everybody in this !@#$% country watch !@#$% cooking shows all night long? No wonder Americans are so FAT!

3. Why are there so many !@#$% hot chicks working out on these fitness commercials? They don't even need to be working out!

4. Why are there so many beer commercials? People would buy beer anyway!

5. Why is everybody dancing all the time on TV?

6. Do these people in all the commercials actually believe all this !@#$% about diets and cars?

7. Where did I put my last Blitz?

8. Why do all these guys drool over women they will never meet or touch?

9. How do all these restaurants stay in business? Sol yawned and blinkd.

10. How many cartoon channels do we...? Sol yawned and blinked and snorted.

11. Sol Yawned and blinked and grabbed a blanket and took a long deep swallow of Blitz.

12. What the h—- does it mean to celebrate diversity? Has anyone ever really thought about what that means? Look! I weigh a pound more than yesterday. I have become even more diverse! Ha! Why don't we talk about multi-beerism?

13. My wife would always ask me what I wanted for Christmas. H—- I'd tell her I needed a new set of screwdrivers, or a hammer, or an oil filter for the truck. So what would I get? A ball cap with deer antlers, or a Blitz beer T shirt, or some knick knack ornament to put on a shelf or some other d—- thing I didn't ask for! Hah! Why didn't I ever get a six pack or even a quart of Blitz? !@#$%! Why didn't I ever get what I wanted? Ever!

Blitz number 14 was nearly gone—the clock was chiming 10:30 am. Old Sol had been through a lot of emotional strain already this Christmas morning. He thought he might cuddle up on the couch with a pillow. "Jeanine, baby, hold me honey, oh, ah, your legs are so silky smooth," mumbled lover boy Sol almost incoherently—and fell asleep in a heap, like a sheep, without a peep, his sorrows to reap.

Such, my friend, was life outside Hollywood. No applause, no redemptive outcome. No sleigh rides, no drummer boys, no group of happy movie stars dancing at the gala event celebrating each other.

No carolers had come to Sol's door Christmas Eve. Nobody walked by and shouted out, "God Bless Ye, Squire Davies. 'Ave a Merry Christmas!" Sol didn't put on a rented Santa suit and carry a giant turkey down to the soup kitchen.

Just another day, and yes, just another emotional beating. A momentary breakdown, yes, but then rigor mortis thankfully returned.

Cheer up, gentle reader. Yes. A new novel had been started! A narrow world, a cold beer, and pleasing nightfall were just a few hours away. Old Sol was sleeping peacefully now.

Then, three black-eyed children suddenly appeared on the patio, peering through the window, quietly watching Sol sleep. "Let us in," they whispered hopefully, comfortably, as if to a parent. "Let us in. We want to use your phone."

But old Sol, dreaming of curvy girls dancing in a beer commercial while a fat guy in a plaid coat and green tie talked about sports and stadium hot dog prices, didn't hear a word.

Johnny Roz and the Boxing Day Way-Early Morning Dream

Christmas night, after returning from a difficult family holiday party, Johnny Roz fell asleep quickly.

Twenty people attended the party. Although he brought presents for every one of his relatives, no one got him anything. Several made fun of his bowl-style haircut.

Kids were screaming, aunts and uncles were fighting over politics, the stereo was blasting away.

Perhaps he had eaten too much ham. Perhaps he had put away too much eggnog. Perhaps the room at eighty-two degrees was too warm.

Whatever. He drank a bottle of Blitz and fell upon his favorite futon, utterly senseless.

His night was to be troubled, creepy, and portentous.

About two am, he began to have a dream; a dream so powerful he flailed his arms and legs wildly about, knocking lamps, clocks, and beer bottles from the tables next to his mattress.

No, the beautiful brunette from down the street did not visit him this night. He was to be haunted by specters terrifying beyond mortal belief!

Behold and Wonder!

At the beginning of his dream, he was driving a Golf Kart through the streets of Hamilton City. Or rather, the Golf Kart was driving him. No matter how hard he tried to steer, the Golf Kart kept heading the same direction—down a one-way brick paved street. At the end of this road, which was strewn with black roses, in a cul-de-sac, were two large warehouses.

There were no windows on either building. One had a single door, the other had a double door. Suddenly cautious, afraid of what might be inside these Giant Mausoleums, he resisted opening the doors. But some unseen force compelled him to look, to see, to discover. Like a salmon swimming up a stream to breed, he was powerless. Boldly, he moved towards the Unknown! Yes.

Hearing loud club mix dance music coming from the building with the single door, he opened it—and was pleased.

He saw over fifty beautiful blond and red-headed young women in bikinis, some topless, all drinking and smiling, laughing, good natured, and at ease. They asked him if he rode a motorcycle—or played in a band—or liked to hunt—or worked on cars. He was attracted to their physiques, yes, but he was thrilled to hear them interested in his life. So many offered him a beer and wanted to give him a back rub. He was handled joyously by so many, so many, over and over.

Then the Golf Kart came in through the door—this was a dream, remember—and angrily nudged him out, out onto the cold street, into the darkness, then guided him towards the other building.

Powerless and weakened, he gazed earnestly at the warehouse with the double doors.

Well, he thought, *things were good in the first building. Maybe something is even better in here.*

Taking a deep breath, he pushed through the double doors. He saw another fifty women, some in hair curlers and pink robes, many texting on smart phones or talking on cell phones, all surrounded by chairs, drawers, tables, big screen TV's and other kinds of social furniture. Many were overweight and angry. None seemed comfortable. Each was wearing a wedding band and a big diamond. Some were pushing shopping carts, or putting gas in an SUV, or talking about restaurants, little league, bunko parties, desserts, Pinterest, and Tupperware.

A large woman with chubby cheeks and big hoop earrings turned and shouted at him, "Why aren't you at work? When are you gonna sell your motorcycle? Why aren't you more like my dad? You !@#$% . You need to spend more time at home. Your belt is the wrong color! You better cancel that deer hunt this weekend! Those clothes look stupid! You loser! Where's the credit card?"

Johnny tried to leave. The Golf Kart blocked the door, wagging its wheels in a threatening manner, growling in an electric voice.

Johnny heard the laughter from the other building, and the music, and smelled the perfume and booze and smokes from across the street. But he wasn't going anywhere. Ever.

Johnny Roz awoke in a cold sweat. He would not sleep again for days. He emptied every bottle of liquor and beer he had in the house and went to early Mass.

Dina and Dolly
Copperfield Gentleman's Club

Two of the lower profile residents of the Hamilton RV Park were Dina and Dolly. The pair, whose gender preference remains a bit unclear, lived in a nice park model with blacked out windows. They were very quiet and actually spent little time at home. Both worked as exotic dancers at the Copperfield Gentleman's Club just outside of town.

Sometimes Sol Davies observed one of the girls coming outside to pick up the newspaper, or dump an ashtray, or get into a car. Or get out of a limo with Canadian plates. But overall, the pair was quite mysterious and was seldom seen in the light of day. Some of the residents considered them snooty.

Not old Sol. Our emerging novelist and cultural analyst was their true friend and faithful defender.

So what if they weren't sociable here in the park, thought Sol—those gals worked hard and provided a valuable service! You don't see them down at the grocery store using food stamps! No sirree, Bob!

Rumor was, Dolly and Dina each had husbands and kids and homes down in Santa Rey, but their professional careers simply didn't match up with the traditional expectations of a wife—like being at home once in a while. Hard to say what their husbands were doing these days, but these gals were making lots of money at the CGC. And loving it. Supposedly, they were spotted by a CGC talent agent at a Super Bowl potluck during the third quarter a few months ago, and, well, the rest was history.

Both of these thirty-five-year-old women were unequivocally hot. Dolly liked to wear tight leather pants and a firm fitting Isotonic-like bustier that nicely accentuated her shape. Her trademark? She wore multi-strap open-toed shoes with six inch heels.

During her regular and robust solo dance routine, she took her leathers off slowly and strutted around the floor in her black fishnet underwear, occasionally draping her most shapely left calf over the shoulder of an unsuspecting connoisseur of the feminine arts and then furtively dangling a most beautiful foot within centimeters of his lap. Wow!

Her sweet sweat invariably puddled on the floor around the percolating patron, and, well, this provocative use of her podiatric peg righteously raked in the dough.

Dina was much more subdued. She typically performed in "casual wear"—like a pink blouse and black slacks. Heaven had been very good to her figure. Once a cheerleader, now an adherent of Yoga, she liked to dance in a more traditional way—wrapping herself around a long, hard, shimmering, brass pole and thrusting her perfectly contoured derriere out toward the audience, moving in time to the steady Boom Chukka Boom, Boom Chukka Boom, Boom Chukka Boom, from the sound systems. Yes. Yes! Her nose was perky, her eyes were bright, and she could "move it." She was sculpted magnificently, and her girl-next-door groovy good looks absolutely drove the greying geezers gonzo. Get this—although it was against the house rules, she enjoyed being spanked—especially during the holidays—by patrons dressed up in green elf outfits. Dina gave and took, gave and took, gave and took …

Wow! A brunette with legs that never quit!

Sometimes the girls danced together—massaging each other's bosoms, squeezing each other's bums, Quebec kissing in the dim light, licking each other's ear lobes, and gyrating wildly, squealing, shrieking, and grunting. Just good harmless fun. Good adult fun. Nothing virtual about that curvy and firm fun reality. Yum.

Like Sol said, these gals worked hard and provided a valuable service. "Hell," said Sol to Adam Swiss, "I know of an art dealer from Toronto, Tom, who flies in once a month just to see those two spank each other!" Just good harmless fun.

Sol decided he should invite Dina and Dolly to the RV Parks New Year's Eve Party... Talk about melting snow! Fire and rain! Wow! Hubba-hubba.

A quick note for future reference. During the last few days, since about the winter equinox, Sol had noticed Leah Free talking to the dancing duo a time or two. All three, dressed in bathrobes and furry slippers, had stood just off the snowy street in front of the park model. "Hmm," mused Sol. "I wonder what that's all about. Maybe they're exchanging recipes!"

Melting Toenail Polish
Adam's Place, December 26th

Even though it was a short winter day, Adam had been busy patching big holes in the street which looped through the park.

His hands were sore, too, from doing a lot of caulking on the Rec Hall doorframe.

But the big caulking job wasn't finished yet.

Coming in late, and tired, he ate some left over Chinese food and took a long, steaming, hot shower. He cleaned himself thoroughly. Everywhere.

Leah, wearing silk pajamas, was painting her toenails, watching TV, and thumbing through a book.

Forty-five minutes later, Adam was enjoying the evening with Leah, who had fallen asleep on the bed, knees up, while reading Fitzgerald's *The Great Gatsby*.

Adam nibbled on her ear lobes—no response.

He stuck his tongue in her rum-flavored belly button—a murmur.

He licked the inside of her cocoanut smelling calves—husky, labored breathing.

He kissed her freshly painted toenails—Bingo!

He looked up, between her perfect knees, and saw her smiling face.

She was smiling because wet toenail polish had smudged his lips. She was not so pleased her paint job had been messed up. Oh well.

Their loving was swift, powerful, epic, and glorious—a locomotive at full throttle, thrashing through the night, trackless and pounding—Fiery Power!

Wintering cardinals, perched on ice-glazed willow branches just outside the trailer, watched through the window, chirping and smiling. Their red heads bobbed, their clutching claws stretched and eased, syncopated. The birds occasionally shrieked with obvious hot-feathered delight.

An early morning sun, a dull red blossom, tired and limp, found Leah and Adam content, cuddling in a pool of molten polish.

Steam curled up out of every un-caulked crack in the travel trailer. Not a bit of ice remained on the windows. Oh My.

Tosh and Tate
Peace in the Pines

Tosh and Tate, a nearing middle-aged couple, lived in an old fashioned doublewide at Space 26. Tosh was a carpenter; he worked with his hands. Some days he found jobs working as a roofer or framer or general laborer. When he was at home working, he had his own playhouse and doghouse handy man building business. The past month or so, Tosh had been busy with Christmas orders.

His wife, a comely and pleasant lady with the most beautiful lips and whitish blonde hair, worked at the nursery located down by the Moonbucks.

The nursery was normally calm this time of year, although Tate had been busy selling a few living Christmas trees.

Leah Free, who bought a fresh floral arrangement for her ladies' book discussion group from the nursery this past summer, was stunned by Tate's beauty. Wow, thought Leah to herself, I wonder if the girl knows what she's got. She has such a pure, virtuous Alpine complexion.

Sometimes Tate played the harmonica down at Moonbucks, to back up Adam Swiss or the nine piece Everyday Band, a Beatles Tribute group famous for their Moonbucks fundraising shows no one attended.

Tate and Tosh cheerfully and faithfully attended St. Arnold's Church on Sundays.

They were a God-fearing couple. They enjoyed living the life they had created, far from their old, anxious world in Arizona. In the evenings, they were energized by constructing a life together, planting dreams, shaping philosophy, loving, and harvesting hope.

Tosh was a lucky man to have such a lovely, loving, supportive wife. And Tate loved her man, a man who was good with his hands and who wanted only the best for his woman.

Such a pretty picture. Tosh builds—Tate nurtures. Tate loves.

Can you do better?

December 28th Amateur Afternoon at the Gentleman's Club
The Worm Turns

As mentioned earlier, Sol had noticed Leah speaking to the exotic dancers Dina and Dolly earlier in the week.

During the rap session—basically just girl talk about movies, Sticky Mart spaghetti noodles, toenail polish, and leg shaving—Leah learned about the Copperfield Gentleman's Club Amateur Dancer show every 28th of the month.

Fully embracing experimentalism, multi-culturalism, and cultural diversity, and believing dancing was an art form, Leah decided to seize the moment and have some fun dancing. Just to be a little naughty. No harm, no foul.

So today, at two pm—exotic dancers worked around the clock, you know—while Adam was out doing some big caulk work around the park, Leah put on new Sticky Mart lacey white lingerie under a robe. Then she headed down to the CGC where she met Dina and Dolly, received instructions, signed a release form, and waited to dance in the nearly-empty venue.

She was given just ten minutes to pole dance on the brightly lit stage.

Leah was told the patrons could not touch her, but they would most likely make inappropriate comments and whistle loudly. Opportunity might knock—sometimes owners of big dance clubs would be in the audience— she might get a chance to land a full-time job and make lots of money.

About 2:17 pm, her chance to go wild came up. The pounding music helped her gyrate and grind against the shiny pole. Flashing lights nearly blinded her—bizarre Clorox-like aromas sickened her. She heard grunts and groans from the invisible audience as she opted for a "Flash Dance" routine and then cheers and applause when she scampered up the brass pole like a chimpanzee.

Her moves were good, but remember, she was an amateur.

Leah noticed her vision was nearly fried; the bright lights were affecting her ability to see. She turned, grabbed the firm and thick shaft in both hands, and thrust and pumped her buttocks out towards the audience, blinking and hoping to regain her sight on the dark side... A cacophonous applause erupted.

"Yeah, BABY!" a Canadian was heard to exclaim. "That's robust and sustainable!"

Then she squealed in near terror. Someone had leaped on the stage and stuck a big fat wad of bills in the stretchy band of her racy, lacy, spacey underwear.

Leah heard that Canadian voice yell out, "Yeah baby, right up the bum!"

She shouted, before turning around, still waiting for her sight to return, "Hey you !@#$%! You can't touch me like that. It's in the rules!"

Turning around, she looked straight into the face of her freakishly-turned on, panting, and drooling—yet estranged—husband, Luther the Churchman.

"I bought this place, baby. My rules now. When are you coming home? Honey, you can dance. By the way, I bought the church, a cosmetics factory, and a board game company. You can have it all, sugar. We can have it all!"

"And get rid of the old piece of !@#$ you've been driving. I bought you a new Mercedes!"

Then he leaned towards her, whispering sweet love nothings in her ear, perhaps recounting the romantic secrets they maintained as a young couple, perhaps reviewing the places they had seen—and touched. His hot breath and low tones got her attention. Her eyes grew wide with wonder, and her heart, swelling, beat a brisk and hopeful jungle rhythm in her heaving breast.

He smiled his old Black Magic smile, handed her a large bath towel and a new credit card, and ambled away, releasing his previously sucked-in gut, eventually opening a mostly-unused side entrance. A shaft of bright, cleansing, and purifying sunlight probed, poked, and prodded Leah's partial nudity.

Luther flipped off the music and the strobes and turned on irritating overhead fifteen hundred watt halogens. "The show is over, boys. Get the hell out. Go home to your wives and kids. Maybe read the Bible or go to church or play a board game! What's wrong with you people, anyway?"

Exit Luther through the door, humming "Battle Hymn of the Republic."

Thirty minutes later, Leah was back at Adam's trailer, sitting placidly in a tub of hot, foamy, and perfumed water, counting the money, fondling her new credit card, and wondering what to do. But she knew what to do.

Then she looked for a suitcase. And found one.

New Year's Eve Party at the RV Park Rec Hall

The NYEP had started innocently enough. About twenty or so of the RV Park residents thought they'd get together in the Rec Hall for a potluck. By word of mouth, emails, and whatever, a menu was more or less put together and the event was on. A few long tables had been set up for the crock pots and ice chests, and several beat-up old Samsonite card tables and chairs dotted the dance floor.

The Widow Douglas had found a box full of seventies-era party favors in her stand-alone metal storage building, and she had placed them festively throughout the hall.

Adam, Zontarg, and the boys were setting up to play a few songs. Another freebie gig, more or less expected from the RV Park working class handy man.

Connie, an always attractive and curvy gal in her late forties, who was married to a highly successful local preacher, was going to sing Patsy Cline songs with the band. Her playlist included "Crazy" and "Walking after Midnight."

A few outsiders slipped through security, including one guy smoking a Camel and wearing a CGC polo shirt. Sol noticed the Canadian limo was parked outside—a few big dudes in overcoats and sunglasses were standing around the back doors. Arnie the Barista and Chip the Bug Man also came to the party, holding hands and cooing. Hard to say who was invited and who just crashed the gate.

Dean Preston from the college—what a windbag—was standing near the vegetable tray, pickled and happy, and leering at women as they passed by. He kept shouting, "Hi baby. I've got a big doctorate in education leadership. Wanna see?" His date for the evening, Counselor Vasquez, had already passed out; she was face down in a bowl of ice cream, hands at her sides, snoring and bubbling, murmuring incoherently about spring break in Mazatlan.

Tosh and Tate peeked in but kept going. "Nothing for us in there," she whispered to her loving man, clutching his hand and affectionately leaning against him. "Let's go find a bowl of good wholesome chili down at the diner!"

Rick and Tracy, a couple from Arizona in town for the Green

Day concert, sat back contentedly on lawn chairs, sipped ice-cold Blitz beers, and laughed at the Big Show. "Honey," whispered Tracy to her husband, "these North New Mexico folks know how to party hearty. Tonight reminds me of Minnesota back in the old days!"

(*Wow*, thought the all-seeing Zontarg, as he scanned the room. *That gal from Arizona is amazingly beautiful. I hear she's super smart, too! But I wouldn't want to get her husband mad at me. That dude looks tough.*)

Man, a lot of drinking was taking place. A lot. Dan the Ice Cream Man was pouring Russian vodka into whatever drinks or glasses he saw unguarded on the tables. Wow. Empty fifth-sized jugs were toppled everywhere.

Time passed—and the place was warming up and cooking.

Phyllis and Willie G, wearing white shirts, ties, and black trousers, and sporting new matching backpacks, stopped in at the party. They delivered some Bible tracts, maps of Ethiopia, and other salvation-related materials.

The happy spiritual couple had driven up to the freshly-caulked Rec Hall in a new covered wagon, pulled confidently by four sombrero-wearing burros.

Phyllis and Willie G were on a New Year's Eve Special Training Mission. They didn't stay long, although Phyllis looked nostalgically at the beer bottles and shot glasses.

New BFF's Leah, Dolly, and Dina started dancing on the tables when AV Allen cranked up the iPod (a club dance music mix) through the band's PA system.

Leah gazed, sadly and knowingly, at Adam Swiss. Then the girls were putting on quite a show. While riding Dina like a Shetland pony, Leah blew Adam a kiss.

Perhaps he noticed, perhaps not.

Adam was duct taping some cables down to the stage, focused on the upcoming show.

He could sense his affair with Leah, all three weeks of it, was over. Just like that.

One of the old park loafers with a big stomach hauled in a portable basketball hoop—so the girls would have a pole for dancing. The booze was flowing pretty vigorously by eight pm, and some wives were taking turns on the pole, too.

The Widow Douglas, a bit chagrined at seeing Chip and Arnie together, and full of Scotch, climbed the poll and ended up sitting in the basket, legs akimbo.

The drinking was too heavy too fast. Some sagged-out old hombre in a Lurk scooter got loopy and drove into a PA stand, knocking over the speaker, which ended up smashing Jann's vintage Ludwig drums. Zontarg and Chip got in a fist fight over Obama care, tax increases, the general decay of the American middle class, the Eurozone, carbon credits, the border fence, climate change, Jody Arias, Rubio, the pending zombie apocalypse, quantitative easing, Egypt, the Cubs, Yogi Berra, drone strikes, Spiderman, James Bond, Chevrolets, bottled water, and Charmain.

The dancing girls were prancing on all fours while the Widow Douglas, who had earlier fallen through the basketball hoop and landed, for a moment, most fulsomely on a smiling Frank Eastermann, spanked them joyfully.

Then the Widow was dancing, too. Then the foursome was a meshed web of kissing and groping. My, my.

Arnie, liquored up early, knocked a Blitz beer keg on its side. The shiny aluminum barrel, apparently with a mind of its own, took off and rolled over Zontarg's vintage Gibson Explorer guitar, smashing the body and electronics.

Fuming, the Angry Z took what was left of the shattered axe and chopped mightily at Chip, and Arnie, the offender.

Chip, tougher than nails, smacked Zontarg on the nose and knocked him out.

Charmain, seeing her man down and bloodied, picked up a PA stand and started swinging, inadvertently striking the legs of the table the four girls were dancing on. They came tumbling down in a gasping, sweaty heap.

"My Fair Ladies!" shouted boozed-up Frank Eastermann, finding a way to trip and fall on the Widow Douglas.

People were cursing and sliding in beer suds.

Dan took his Beijing bass and ran out to the relative safety of the ice cream truck.

Contento, after picking up his dented Zildjian cymbals and surveying the damage to his drum kit, said simply to Swiss—

"I'm done. Don't call me anymore about these goofy projects."

Meanwhile, rolling over, the lithe, lovely, and lean Leah saw her husband come through the door, long and leggy girlfriend Kat in tow. Mrs. Free pitched a fifth of Jim Beam at Luther. It missed but struck Van Dorn in the belly, knocking the wind out of her. She collapsed into a heap, nose first, splashing into a frothy, foaming, and fizzy phantasm of Blitz.

For a moment, time stopped. Leah and Luther smiled at each other. She was coy. He was sly. They knew. His wallet was thick and bulging, outlined courageously in his tight back pocket. She was transfixed by the wallet. They understood.

Luther eased the gasping Van Dorn to her feet and took her home. Game Over.

The hot and perfectly-hipped Widow, after struggling to get away from Eastermann, ended up at Sol Davie's feet. He helped her up, enjoying the curves of her waist and bottom as his hands wandered knowingly, quickly, and hopefully. Her fishnet hose were tattered, but her legs were firm and inviting. So firm.

Moments later, Sol Davies and the Widow were hugging and kissing fervently, standing in a fragrant pool of freezing Blitz beer. Holding his round faced in her hands and withdrawing her pointed, lizard-like, and wet tongue from his mouth, the Widow cried out with great and honest passion—"Oh, Sol, you old goat, I've waited so long for you—dontcha know I love you, baby?"

Sol felt an excitement rising—something he hadn't known for years.

But Sol had to know, "What about Chip? What's going on with Chip?"

"Oh, h——, Sol, Chip and I had it going on, big time, for a while. That kid can rock. But he can't roll. Happily, he realized he was gay. And now, well, it's Chip and Arnie, you know, the young Barista from Moonbucks! They make a great couple and love each other with gusto, completely, sincerely, and honestly! Chip's got a big brassy wand and a hairy chest, but believe me, you hunk of burning love, that's about all he's got. He's no Sol Davies, for d—— sure."

Sol happily reached out and squeezed her aged-yet-great-and-perfect bosom with both of his big calloused hands, glad he hadn't published his book on women yet and smiled, "Happy New Year,

Jeanine honey. This will be the best year of our lives! You make my heart sing." She squealed with hungry anticipation.

Within thirty minutes, they were making banshee-screaming love, scattering pink, red, and ivory rose petals on the never-been-waxed linoleum floor of his living room—two old people loving in the RV Park, laughing and carrying on like there were many tomorrows.

Bulletin: Sol's notes on women would be temporarily relegated to his 'poetry of portfolio' collection—that which was produced without thoughts of publication!

Years later, soaked in marital happiness, Sol would burn that emerging inappropriate and politically incorrect tome in the fireplace when Jeanine wasn't looking. Good call.

The NEYP Amps UP!

The NYEP had become a riot. Holiday cheer and good feeling had been replaced by kicking, eye-gouging, crotch-kneeing, screaming, gut-punching, unhealthy grunting, rumbling, guzzling, and vomiting—an orgy of drunken violence.

Swiss grabbed his guitar, which was thankfully still in its hard case, and a nearly-full bottle of vodka, and then headed back to his trailer, just as Hamilton City PD was pulling into the park.

Leah was not in the trailer when he got there.

Adam noticed his loyal DT-1 was waiting for him patiently.

Under a streetlamp, just across Edison Avenue, Preacher Hoss, whose beard was somehow blue again, Phyllis, and Willie G, were conducting an impromptu Bible study with some of the retreating revelers. The three black-eyed children were reading Ezekiel—and pointing at the stars.

Father Deerjohn, driving by the small group as he made yet another trip to Nebraska for a funeral, shook his head sadly. He muttered woefully, "Protestants!"

Our Couple No One Yet Knew—Elvis and the Lovely Tattooed

Lady—out for their evening walk down to the diner, arms lovingly around each others' waists, paid no attention to the melee'.

How large must the world be? How much entertainment do we truly require? Why bother with nothing?

The three black-eyed children watched the police enter the Rec Hall and make a few arrests.

This NYEP was finished, spent, wasted. The arrival of HC Police had caused an abrupt end to the Fighting Festival.

Party goers streamed out of the building, carrying ice chests, chairs, broken arms, bad memories, and bottles. A few were led out in handcuffs by Officers Turcotte, Westerman, and Hoyt.

Oh, the arrestees' names were not revealed pending the dispensation of court cases.

By 11:30 pm, New Year's Eve, the party was over. Everyone was either at home sick, in jail, or in the emergency room. Happy New Year!

Denouement
My Baby Sent Me a Letter

A few days passed. Tough days for Adam. Strange days for Mrs. Free.

As it turned out, Mr. and Mrs. Luther Free actually owned the travel trailer Swiss had been renting.

Interesting, don't you think? Or simply random?

On the twelfth of January, Swiss received a "tracked" letter from Leah. She had spent $4.70 on postage, so Adam decided he'd better open the envelope. Inside he found a tear-stained letter, and official paperwork giving him full title to his travel trailer:

Dear Adam,

You are a great guy, a fair lover, and an okay musician. Sometimes you sing off key.

There isn't much for me to say, honey.

Things are back to normal, I guess, and Luther and I are working on our relationship. He wants me to seek counseling to figure out what's wrong with me.

We have returned to our regular routine of church, Scrabble night, and softball. He is getting even fatter but has upped my expense allowance.

I am attending Bible studies at a place called the Daughters of Ethiop Temple in hopes of finding myself.

Luther was suspicious until he learned Preacher Hoss, the Pastor of Just DOET, was a Scrabble player. Now Preacher Hoss has joined the weekly Scrabble games at our house. I don't like the way he looks at my behind, though.

I enjoyed our little wild time, but you can't expect me to leave Luther and the boys for a life as a handy man's woman. Please lose my number. Please don't take it personally. Since time began, women have always sought the "best fit" males for their mates—big muscles, big wallets, or clever minds, or with superior hunting-gathering ability.

My personal genetic pool cries out for a man with a big bank account. And despite his many failings, yes, Luther has dough.

Oh, don't look for me in my worn-out old Lexus anymore. I am driving my brand-new silver Mercedes SUV these days. Plus, Luther told me I could be a VP in his company. Could you do that for me? No. All I did for you was cook spaghetti noodles, dust your dumpy little place, and wait for you to come home and make savage and fulfilling love to me. What's love got to do with shopping?

Luther has employed some disaster restoration company to fix the Rec Hall. Your big NYEP completely trashed the place. But you won't have to do any of the work.

We have retained a pricey and high-powered law firm from Sioux City, Iowa to deal with the assault charges Luther's ex-girlfriend, that s—— Kat Van Dorn, has brought against me. Seems my whiskey bottle did some damage to her liver. Probably wasn't the first time.

My mom is living with us permanently now and she is taking care of Mike, Chip, and Ernie, my three sons. This will free me up to do more meditating and toenail polishing.

Did I tell you I read an article about how women don't completely understand their important and powerful husbands?

Oh—enclosed please find the title to your trailer—Luther wants you to have it. Strange he is giving it to you instead of trying to sell it. You might want to caulk a few of the seams—I thought it was pretty drafty in there and always chilly. You spend a lot of time caulking holes in the RV Park—maybe you should apply some caulk to your own cracks.

Maybe your heart needs some caulk, but I don't know how to squeeze the trigger anymore. Sorry, baby. I just can't pull the trigger.

I guess I will have to unfriend you from Facebook. Oh, I forgot. You don't have a computer or a phone.

Oh, Luther told me he will be selling the RV Park to Copperfield Community College later this spring.

That's where I got my BA degree and where Luther got his ex-girlfriend Kat Van Dorn. What a d— w— she is. Stupid liver.

The college is giving him sixteen million for the RV Park—about sixteen million more than it's worth, but it's only tax payer money, so what. Whatever. Luther says Copperfield is run by idiots, and he should know.

The college wants to use the trailers for extended student housing and to further celebrate community and lifelong diversity. You might want to move your drafty trailer out of there before the parties start up. I know you are basically a quiet and introverted fellow. It's just too bad you don't have a real job or more ambition.

Luther is so smart and actually you are not. Ha. Love you baby. I am going to shave my legs later—wish you could watch. Not really.

What did my mom say? Fall in love with an artist or musician or dancer but marry a doctor or lawyer or engineer or some kind of rich guy. Whatever. You're not actually a musician, just a handy man who can strum a few chords and who tries to sing poetic ideas. So what was I thinking? Sniff. Miss you baby. Take care of your caulk gun. Sometimes it drips and leaves a mess.

By the way—concerning your song about the middle class star you sing all the time at Moonbucks. I am not in the middle class and neither are you. You are a poor handy man and I've got money. So you might want to change those words. And I'm not afraid of happiness, either. Mind your own business.

Formerly Yours for a Beautiful and nearly Perfect Nineteen Days,

Respectfully

Mrs. Leah Free.

PS—please tell Dina and Dolly thanks for the memories.

Those girls know a lot more about life than we understand. They are like philosophers or something.

Maybe more later but probably not. By the way, toenail polish takes about two hours to dry properly. And tell Jann he will be receiving some new DW drums from Luther's Music Store, so don't be surprised if a Rocking Luther's Mad Music van pulls up in front of his place. Zontarg and his bass player buddy are crazy, baby. Charmain needs therapy. You can do better.

PPS. I loved it when you poured rum in my navel and licked it out drop by drop. I told Luther about our fun little trick, and he says we'll try it out soon. But he doesn't drink, so we'll use lemonade or fruit juice or something that might get sticky. Thanks for the idea. Yum. I get excited just thinking about it now.

PPPS. Oh. Why don't you buy yourself a new motorcycle? Oh, I forgot. You don't have any money. Luther says we might get a Load King.

One more thing, Adam Swiss. I know what I want. Do you?

Wrap Up

Spring finally came to Hamilton City. What happened? What did we learn?

Adam Swiss employed Frank Eastermann to tow his travel trailer over to Concho, Arizona. Seems an old friend of Adam's from Crete College had a vacant lot, with utilities, where Swiss could park his tired old unit for good.

Adam didn't want to ride his DT-1 over to Concho. He and Eastermann found a way to get his faithful and loving companion inside the travel trailer. They drained the gas and oil and then carefully placed the Yamaha on Swiss' bed. Swiss covered the old girl with a blanket.

So Swiss moved out to Apache County on April first.

Eastermann and Johnny Roz became pretty good friends and could be seen playing checkers together every few days in Streeter's Park. No romance here—just two dignified gentlemen who gracefully accepted life without the entanglements of female companionship—real or imagined.

Phyllis and her skinny husband were last seen in their covered wagon heading east down the shoulder of I-80 somewhere near

Lexington, Nebraska. Quite a rig.

They had a picture of President Obama on the south side of the wagon, and a picture of Governor Romney on the north. On the top, facing heavenward, was an image of Preacher Hoss in a blue beard.

Each night, Phyllis and Willie G had a robust romantic interlude lasting about four hours. The burros, who all knelt gently in alfalfa, corn, or broom grass, when the sun vanished, continuously watched and wondered at the commotion. Crazy people, they thought, munching on feed and resting.

Amazingly, Phyllis was down to about one-hundred thirty-five pounds and now wears size eight pants. She had been working out at gyms along the way. Willie G, who saw himself as the luckiest mannequin in the world, was quite pleased he and the wife got religion and were now travelling down the open road to Omaha.

Three black-eyed children, wearing tin foil boat-shaped hats, were plodding along behind them. One of the children was carrying a Scottish flag. They each wore black pants and white shirts and carried backpacks.

A slender man in a black hat, just out of their sight, followed the missionaries, lurching in and out of trees and shrubbery. Some believed he had tentacles.

None of the Omaha-bound pilgrims could see the I-S drone surveillance aircraft, flying overhead at about 10,000 feet, which was tracking their movements and listening to their tax-exempt conversations.

In other news—

Chip and Arnie were married in California at a private Disk-Knee Land ceremony and then moved to Colorado and opened up a Head Shop. Business is smokin'!

What brought them together? Well, after Willie G left to become a missionary, the Espressions store had an opening for a living mannequin. Arnie took the job to supplement his income.

One day, when Arnie was modeling a very tight Speedo, Chip, who was spraying bug killer around the building foundation outside the window, noticed Arnie and his svelte and silky man-moves. They met for coffee at Moonbucks later, and, well...

Over in Colorado now, Chip did a little bug exterminating on the side. He occasionally thought of the Widow's firm legs, but only in a platonic manner. "She was a nice lady, Arnie. Almost like a mom to me. That's all!"

Arnie's own frisky mom converted to Catholicism and now attended Mass daily at St. Arnold's. She found peace with her husband, but not love. She has considered taking Orders.

Earl sure missed Arnie, his beer drinking buddy, but he really liked his new son-in-law, who also enjoyed drinking Blitz. This threesome had a rollicking great time when the boys came home to visit.

Earl was now taking classes at Copperfield Community College so he could become a certified massage therapist. He had a crush on a big-bosomed red-headed gal who worked in the convenience store in Hamilton City.

Whatever. Get in line, Earl.

When the residents of the RV Park learned they were to be evicted by the community college, a huge riot broke out and the Rec Hall was destroyed once again. But Luther had it rebuilt for the second time in six months, with help from Preacher Hoss and the Just Daughters of Ethiop Temple Foundation.

President Phil Dolly from Copperfield Community College, the county's largest postsecondary institution, concerned about his and the school's image following the riots, did his best to bring healing to Hamilton City.

"Yes," said Dolly in a televised press conference, "Let the healing process begin. Our thoughts and prayers go out to those RV Park Residents who have lost their homes and livelihoods to this unfortunate man-made disaster.

"But yet, in some small way, as we begin the rebuilding process, perhaps social justice has been served!

"I am calling for a complete investigation by local, state, and federal agencies to determine the cause of this conflagration. We are one Copperfield, one Hamilton City, one RV Park—a diverse but vibrant community committed to a focused mission, better lives for our students. We are a family, and families go through trying times, yes, kaff, kaff, as we move into a robust twenty-first century filled with challenges and opportunities, our partnerships must be nourished by our commitment to quality and feedback assessments and the six-year period it takes to complete one-semester certificates!"

After the "Rec Hall Riot of 2012," as the event became known on cable news, Dolly had several counselors work on site to help displaced trailer people develop strategic goals for their future lives and life-long learning cohorts.

Counselor Elena Vasquez took the lead in this healing process, which the college deemed a "successful partnership with those diverse community stakeholders who find themselves displaced by man made disasters and the emergent and focused group-approved needs of the higher education teaching-learning process."

Whatever. If you don't understand all this stakeholder and partnership and diversity stuff, don't feel too bad.

The people who work at colleges don't know what it means, either. But it sounded good—at least to them. You might say such philosophical compost gave meaning to their work—or gave them something to do.

Interestingly enough, loping and bulging Zontarg, who was lurching around the burned out, broken down, busted up RV Park looking for usable trash, caught the immediate and hopeful attention of beauteous and fiery Counselor Vasquez during one of her on site visits. *Yum*, the smoldering young woman thought to herself. *Haven't I seen that hunk of burning love somewhere before? That's one stakeholder I'd like to get to know better. What a steak! Hot d——-!*

The old-time residents finally gave up, ran up the white flag and left, or pulled out their RV's, Lurk scooters, and trailers, and went on to better or at least different lives.

"And they call that !@#$% Copperfield a College. I wouldn't hire that idiot President Dolly to mow my lawn!" said Cay, a ghost-pepper-hot seventy-two-year-old stripper with great legs, who had just returned from vacationing in Arizona. Lovely Cay was cradling her dog Mocha and on her way out of the shambles and on to Quebec.

Speaking of changing addresses, Dina and Dolly eventually moved into the Luther Free mansion. They worked as nannies and life coaches. They were certainly teaching Mike, Chip, and Ernie a few things about life. Luther had been reading the Bible with the girls late at night. Luther was also contemplating installing a lovely brass pole for dancing down in the basement.

Val Hamilton and the Paint Girl got together quietly. They built an A frame house on the outskirts of town and were quite happy. In the daytime, she painted North New Mexico landscapes from the upper balcony, and Val continued to write novels few people read. Sometimes he watched her stir a can of paint just to find the right kind of inspiration before writing.

At night, every night, they made honey sweet love—furiously. Funneled passions swirled like primer and pigment. Wow. Some like it hot. Some like it colored.

Prof Van Dorn dropped all of her lawsuits. She returned to the academic life and drank only light beer at college staff happy hours once a month. At the present time, she was cohabitating with one Dr. Salinas Chick, a pot-bellied but stable old humanities professor who enjoyed Chinese takeout and black and white classic movies. He owned five cats and a small run-down house, but she was pleased with his calm and steady commitment to her and her legs. Kat's liver was better, and she found a good life away from the buzz of business and drama.

Sometimes Kat wondered why she found soft and physically unfit men attractive.

Whatever floats your boat, honey. More power to you. At least one boozing outlier in this crazy play eventually found happiness.

Speaking of joy, the couples who were solid and happy at the beginning of December were still happy. How much drama do we need in our lives?

Concerning happiness—Old Sol and the Widow were blissful. Perhaps good things do come to those who wait. He cut back on TV watching and was getting back into shape. Sol genuinely loved and respected Jeanine and her three too-cute Beagle puppies. The Widow looked great still, and Sol loved to watch her shave those silky legs.

Although barely relevant to this tale, you should know McDougal, the former socialist and current hamburger king, had been told by his doctor to lay off the red meat and fries.

By the way, the old militant socialist had caught a glimpse of Phyllis Swiss when she first came to town looking for Adam, but his desire came too late. Ach. "Oh, laddie, that der big woman is a looker!" he said to Johnny Roz when the dreamer boy was enjoying a burger one Saturday afternoon. Yes, just too, too late. Her marriage to Willie G took her off the market. Too bad she didn't have a twin. Yum.

Charmain and Buzz and the Random Chick (turned out she played drums) and Zontarg and Dandy D were all living together in Zontarg's new recording studio he built out of usable building materials reclaimed from the "Rec Hall Riot of 2012." Zontarg, Random, and Dandy Dan had formed a power trio. This new band was ready for a break out. They hadn't finalized their play list yet, though.

And—Preacher Hoss finally revealed his great singing voice and would audition for the new band later in the summer.

Wait, there's more! To celebrate their happy reunion and Mother's Day, Luther and Leah Free took a two-week cruise off the California and Baja coasts in early May. Even though the weather was quite warm, Mrs. Free spent most of the trip below deck in their cabin, wrapped up in a blanket. Luther found a great bunch of board game playing guys from jovial Malibu to keep him company while his wife was "resting."

In fourteen days, Leah came above deck three times. She would shade her eyes and look to the east, sniffle, and return to her warm bed below, frequently overwhelmed by fits of crying.

Leah had not painted her toenails since the morning of December 31st.

Fini: Adam Swiss Considers Architecture of the DT-1

A few months later, on his way home from Payson one summer evening, heading to his travel trailer in Concho:

Tired Swiss, rattling along on his aging Yamaha,

Passed four bikes—three Dyna-glides and a modern-day Indian on the long hill approaching Woods Canyon Lake.

The riders were typical—doo rags, chaps, tats, vests, boots sprawled on forward controls.

Their passengers—lovely, fully-kitted long-legged women—one looked like

Leah—wearing fashionable shades, spiked boots, charming tube tops, Motor Company bandinis—were hugging the tough guys.

The Bikes were nothing. The Women were fetching—like always.

An hour later, Swiss sat on a white plastic chair, gazing at the still-cooling engine of his tired old DT-1, which was glowing dimly in the yellow bug-resisting light.

A half-empty bottle of good Scotch was perched on the steps to his travel trailer...

And it came to him like so many lightning bugs.

Yes, the women were lovely. Yes the tats and clothes were noticeable.

But when you distill things down to the truth...

It's the architecture—not the culture—women were a kind of social furniture, too. Graceful and shapely, they had purpose.

But the purpose escaped him. Or "It" simply eluded him. Over and over again.

"The Elusive It!" thought Swiss. "What was 'It'?"

What meant anything? Big Cars?

Big Twins? Big Racks?

His Yamaha clinked as it cooled. The beat-up Enduro had been a good friend—constant and loving. Swiss turned off the bug lamp and felt as Free ever.

Women weren't treacherous. They were women. And his motorcycle? Always waiting for him serenely. Constant. No complaints, no politics, no jealousy, no...

religion, no need for therapy, no drama. Add some oil, tighten the chain, and use a little polish. No problems.

He wondered what Leah was doing with Luther. Right then, right now, right there, beneath the slow, heavy, pock-marked and dripping moon in Hamilton City.

A Thunderstorm blew up from over the rim and made waves on Concho Lake. He shut the windows, glad he had caulked the leaky seams at last.

In the still air of the trailer, he could smell her toenail polish—lingering even though so many months had passed since she had been there.

"Miss you, baby," he said at last to no one, not even to the squirrels outside in the trees, then turned out the light and rolled over on a chilling bed. Free at last.

Adam whispered in the dark—"Who knows what you want, Leah. I don't want anything. I already have it."

Our Main Character Revealed!

A Yamaha DT-1 250 Motorcycle much like Adam's.

About the Author

Jeffrey Ross, who resides in Arizona, is a writer, rockabilly musician, and former full-time community college teacher. He has had four "Views" pieces published on *InsidehigherEd.com*, has authored and co-authored several national and international op-ed articles on community college identity, purpose, and culture, and has recently published numerous parody poems and articles on the *Cronk News* higher education satire website. Ross co-authored the comic and critically acclaimed campus novel *College Leadership Crisis: The Philip Dolly Affair* (Rogue Phoenix Press, 2011).

Also by Jeffrey Ross
at
Rogue Phoenix Press

College Leadership Crisis: The Phillip Dolly Affair is literary in development but grounded in "chaotic" community college daily experience. The novel is comic, satiric, quasi-politically correct, edgy, and richly descriptive of community college life, leadership foibles, and cultural themes. This hyperbolic text is entertaining, edifying, and fun. Little community college fiction—comic or otherwise—exists—the authors are fearless in their humorous—and sometimes biting—analysis of community college culture....

The "stereotype-busting" authors reacquaint readers with the [faded] ideals of the 1960's social renaissance.

While community colleges are currently receiving heightened attention, this novel provides a behind-the-scenes analysis of many "whispered truths," those simmering but unspoken workplace issues, behaviors, and machinations nearly every worker (Everyman) in America will recognize.

Leah Wescott, Editor of *Cronk News* says about *College Leadership Crisis: The Phillip Dolly Affair*:

I was most drawn to the descriptions (regardless of genre) of the no-win conflict real life community colleges face between missions of vocational preparation and ambitions of higher learning. Both visions are ridiculed brilliantly though neither is without merit. Faculty, staff, students and townies are also held under the humor microscope. There's plenty to laugh and cry about as you recognize your community and yourself.

Photo Credits

Title Page: photo courtesy Julie Sego

New Year's Eve Party: photo courtesy Tracy Lambrecht

Yamaha DT-1 250 Motorcycle: photo courtesy Yamaha Motor Corp.

VISIT OUR WEBSITE
FOR THE FULL INVENTORY
OF QUALITY BOOKS:

http://www.roguephoenixpress.com

Representing Excellence in Publishing

Quality trade paperbacks and downloads

in multiple formats,

in genres ranging from historical to contemporary romance, mystery and science fiction.

Visit the website then bookmark it.

We add new titles each month!